The Black Rose Murders

The Penny Detective 10

John Tallon Jones

D1715922

Published by G-L-R (Great Little Read)

Copyright John Tallon Jones

Other books in the Penny Detective series

PROLOGUE

The Excelsior Hotel Paris: **summer 1985**

Even though it was unusually cold outside for the time of the year, Harper was sweating with nervous tension. Examining the disguise in the bathroom mirror, it seems to be perfect but in situations like these, you could never tell if every angle had been covered. The slightly used black and white clothing painted just the right picture, and the false metal rimmed glasses that Rudi had suggested were the perfect finishing touch. Harper was nervous and knew that the next couple of hours were going to be potentially life threatening. The people gathered in conference room number six would kill without a second thought, but that was the sort of risk that made life worth living, and the rewards made up for the danger. If these men were as professional as Rudi claimed, then they would have meticulously checked out the room for any listening device as a normal part of their routine, so that's why it had to be like this. It was dangerous, but also deliciously exciting

Harper walked into the bedroom and looked at the food trolley with the white linen cloth draped over it. As an idea, the plan was far from original. In fact, Rudi had got it from an obscure espionage book he had once read. If the people in conference room six had read the same book, there could be problems. Harper lifted up the cloth and activated the miniature listening device with the tiny but powerful microphone strapped to one of the support legs, then let the pristine white linen fall back into place.

It was time to go.

Five minutes later, there it was. Conference room six. There must be no hesitation now, or the adrenalin levels would drop, and it would be finished.

A loud decisive knock on the door, confident smile, and then wait.

A voice from inside called out loudly "Who is it?"

Harper replied in perfect French. "Service d'étage, monsieur."

The door opened slightly, and a pair of steely grey eyes looked out through the crack.

"We never ordered room service; you must have made a mistake."

Harper changed the language to English with a heavy French accent. "No mistake, sir; conference room number six, club sandwiches and champagne, compliments of the hotel."

"Wait."

The door closed, and Harper was left alone in the corridor with no other alternative other than to stand there and sweat. It was almost five minutes before the door opened again. A huge gorilla of a man with a humourless face stepped to one side and said, "Come."

Harper wheeled the trolley inside. There were four men and a woman sitting around a table. They continued to talk and never looked at the trolley. The man, who had opened the door, looked like the hired muscle of the operation. He came over and examined the food and drink. A distraction was needed and quickly.

"I have this, which explains clearly that it is complementary and that you don't have to pay, sir."

The gorilla left the examination of the trolley, took the note and read it.

"What's your name?"

"Harper, sir."

"Well, Harper, make sure that we don't have any more disturbances until we leave in about..." He made a play of looking at his expensive gold wristwatch. "In about two hours."

He handed Harper some French Francs and smiled coldly.

"Yes, sir; if there is anything else that you require, don't hesitate to call room service."

The gorilla nodded impatiently, and Harper headed for the exit. Outside in the corridor, the walk to the lift could have been interrupted at any time with a bullet to the back of the head. The temptation to run was overpowering but resisted.

Back in the bedroom, the attention was focused on a small black metal device lying on the coffee table. It was a Sony receiver-recorder and was about the same size as a shoebox. There was already a two-hour tape inside, which Rudi had inserted beforehand. Harper turned the volume up and put the headphones on. The voices of the people in the conference room could clearly be heard. Game on!

Three hours later Rudi and Harper were in the back of a taxi speeding towards the airport. The plan though improvised had been a complete success. They now had enough information stored on the cassette to initiate stage two and make a lot of money. The next stage was the best part; arranging a fee with the prey for keeping their mouths shut about the information that they now held.

It was when they got out of the taxi and were making their way into the terminal building that Rudi saw her. The woman from the conference room was getting out of a huge Peugeot. Rudi cursed softly under his breath. Things hadn't gone as smoothly as he had thought. This was a problem that had to be dealt with immediately. He looked at his watch and nodded to Harper to carry on walking.

While Harper headed for Departures, Rudi hid at the side of the sliding doors waiting for the lady to appear. She came through the doors in a hurry and looked around frantically. He stepped out and slipped his arm through hers, turned and walked her forcefully and quickly back into the car park.

He leaned down and whispered menacingly in her ear. "We need to talk, Madame. Shall we go somewhere quieter?"

CHAPTER ONE

Summer 1987

I had never been inside a golf club before but I was already impressed by the standard of cars in the car park. I stuck my Riley Elf in between a Porsche 911 and a Mercedes 300D, stepped out onto the crisp white gravel, and buttoned up my tie. I stuck my trilby over my shaved bald head, to make myself seem less aggressive and walked past the seventeenth and eighteenth holes heading for the reception.

The man at the reception desk looked at me as if I had just burnt his house down and made love to his wife. He had an air of upper – class arrogance about him that I could respect. He slightly brightened when I told him that I had an appointment with Henry Green, and told me that I could probably find him in the clubhouse bar. I made my way through a cobbled courtyard. At the far side, there was an ornate wooden bridge over a stream and a path that took you past a lake, which had a 'NO FISHING' sign painted on a wooden notice board. The people that I passed were mainly old and attached to golf trolleys as they stumbled their way to the practice putting greens or the first hole, which started near the clubhouse door.

There was only one man in the bar area, and I instinctively knew it was him. He had the look of new money about him, the sort of person who had clawed his way to the top of the heap. He must have been in his mid-fifties, and his face and body showed signs of alcohol abuse and unhealthy eating habits. He wore a loose fitting Ben Sherman shirt, and beige chinos that I suspected were designed to hide his fat beer gut. His eyes were bloodshot blue and penetrating, and when I approached the table, he shot out of his chair and pumped my hand like he expected water to come out of my mouth. He must have recognised me too because having an appointment with him was the only way I could have ever been allowed into this place in the battered off-the-peg suit I was wearing.

"You must be Morris Shannon."

I agreed with him that I had to be, and noticed that his accent was Yorkshire, with a trace of something else that I couldn't identify.

"I'm glad that you could make it." He patted my shoulder and indicated that I had his permission to sit down.

"Can I get you something? The special plate is Lancashire Hotpot or they do an acceptable Cottage Pie."

"Thanks, Mr Green, but I've already eaten. Maybe a drink of something?"

He clicked his fingers like a Sultan, and as if by magic a waiter appeared, though not out of a bottle. "Two single malts, and some nibbles, Stevens." The man disappeared with impeccable stealth, and I hoped that he was going to come back with the good stuff.

"So, how much do you want to get my daughter back, Mr Shannon?" He was straight to the point and obviously didn't believe in idle chat with riff-raff like me.

"Like I told you on the phone, sir, if your daughter doesn't want to come back because she is over eighteen, there is not a lot that I can do."

The whisky and snacks arrived, and he waited, for me to pick up my glass and take a sip before he continued. "That's a nice single malt, what is it?"

He looked pleased as if he had distilled the stuff himself. "It's a sixteen-year-old Glenlivet Nadurra. It is my personal stock. I'm glad that you approve." I could see by the look on his face that he wasn't being condescending, but was like me, a fan of good whisky.

He took a sip himself and turned his eyes on me. "Ok, Mr Shannon, maybe I put it the wrong way when I phoned you. I know I can't force her to do anything, but I can stop her from ruining her life, by spending it with this man. I want to protect her from herself."

"You mean that you want me to dig up dirt on her man friend."

"This man friend as you call him is not what he claims to be. I'm sure of it. He says that he is an American, but is very vague about where he was brought up. I also know for a fact that the police are very interested in him."

"And does your daughter know about this?

"If Kristie does, she is keeping it to herself."

"So how do you know?"

"I followed them to a hotel in Chester and confronted him."

"Do you make a habit of following you daughter, Mr Green?"

"Only when I think that somebody is going to take advantage of her. This Ashton character had booked them into a hotel; all that I wanted to do was tell her not to cheapen herself."

"So that still doesn't answer my question about how you know that the police are interested in Ashton."

"Because when they took me to the police station, they implied it."

"Let me get this straight, Mr Green. You were arrested in Chester by the police?"

"No, I wasn't charged with anything, I was let off with a caution. I had been trying to reason with Kristie, and things got a little bit heated. Some punches were thrown, and the police arrived. They seemed to think it was my fault."

"And was it?"

"I was just doing what any responsible father would do in the circumstances. Have you got children, Mr Shannon?"

I shook my head.

"Well, when you do, maybe you will understand what I mean. You bring them up, care for them, give them the best, and then some little turd comes along and ruins their life."

"So when you were held by the police. What did they say about Ashton?"

"They didn't tell me anything directly; it was just that they appeared so quickly, and when I was at the police station they asked me a lot of questions about him, and especially how come he had so much money."

"So Ashton has a lot of money?"

"On the surface, it certainly looks that way, but he doesn't seem to have a job and is very vague about where he gets it from."

"He could have inherited it."

Green found this funny and didn't think it justified an answer. "The reason that I am so worried, is that the police also asked me questions about Kristie, you understand the implication? If he is a criminal, then she could be implicated."

"But they let you off?"

"Yes, yes, but that's not the point, man. The point is that after the episode with the police, I understood that I needed to buy somebody who could do the dirty work that I was trying to do. That's why I want to purchase you, Mr Shannon."

Green couldn't see the arrogance of his last remark. I guess that with his money, he was used to acquiring whatever he needed, and that included peasants like me. I wasn't offended; I just made a mental note to increase the fee I was going to charge him. "I'm not really for sale, Mr Green, but you can hire my services on a daily basis for a set fee plus expenses. What sort of a girl is Kristie?"

My question seemed to confuse him as if he had never really thought about it before. "She's great," he said, snapping his fingers again for the waiter to bring us two more whiskies. "She's been sheltered, and that's probably my fault. For the last few years, she

has spent more and more time staying at my sister Verna's house.

Verna was a wild one herself when she was that age; I think she

could have done more to have curbed my daughter's freedom. We all

need to have some boundaries, don't you think? Kristie doesn't

understand the real world, and with this man, she can't possibly

realise what situation she is getting herself into. I tried to reason with

her the other night, but she wouldn't listen. She told me to mind my

own business, and that it was her life."

"So what do you think is the attraction that she has for Ashton?"

"That's why I want to buy........" he smiled, "Sorry, hire you to

find out. He is old enough to be her father. She is certainly not

attracted to his money, because I have enough of that, and she has as

much as she needs."

"As we are talking about money, Mr Green." I went into my

pocket, brought out a sheet of paper and slid it across the table to

him. "This is what I charge, plus daily expenses."

He examined the paper carefully. "You're not cheap, Mr Shannon."

"Is that what you are looking for? A bargain detective? I'm sure that you can find loads of them in the Yellow Pages."

"No, I never said that I didn't want to hire you, I was just making a comment that I am surprised that you sort of people earn so much."

"My sort of people, Mr Green, often work in dangerous conditions, and can come up against some pretty nasty people. Besides, you are paying for two detectives. That's me and my partner."

He went into his pocket, brought out his wallet, took out some cash and passed it over. "Is that enough to be going on with?"

It certainly was. It meant that I could put petrol in my car and eat. I tried to keep the happiness out of my voice. "You will get a full written report about what I have done and what expenses I have incurred," I added just to make sure that he had understood. "The expenses are extra."

The drinks arrived, and I was pleased to note that they were doubles. He picked up his glass and downed half in one gulp, then trained those blue eyes on me again. "I expect that you will find out as much information as you can, about who Ashton Baxter is, and how he makes his money. I also want to know why he came to Croxley and in what way are the police interested in him. Is that clear?"

"Couldn't be clearer, sir."

I got out my notebook and took down some more details. I was surprised as they had only been going out with each other for a short while that Green was so worried, but I didn't push it. When I came to the question about Kristie's mother, it seemed to bother him. "She's not around anymore."

Now, what the hell did he mean by that? "Can you give me a few more details, Mr Green?"

"She died, about four years ago."

"And Kristie? How old is she?"

"She will be 27, no 28, in January."

"Did she take her mother's death, hard?"

"I don't think that she ever got over it. Maybe this is the reason why she is so vulnerable and such easy prey to someone like Ashton."

I asked him a few more questions, said I would be in touch and left. On the surface, it seemed easy money for the work I had to do. I suspected that Green was being a heavy-handed father and that his opinion of Ashton was misplaced. I fired up the Elf and made my way to the pub to meet my best friend and partner, Shoddy, to see what he made of it.

CHAPTER TWO

The place that was near enough a second home to me was a pub close to my flat called The Old One Hundred. It's not what you would call fashionable, but is a serious drinking establishment full of mostly down and outs. You are hit with the aggressive vibe the moment you enter the bar area, and if you are a newcomer, it's best to avoid eye contact to lower the risk being assaulted. This is especially true at closing time when drink levels are high and often spark a mass brawl in the wink of an eye. You get the impression that the landlord, Bill is happy to see the back of his customers and treats every day without violence as a bonus. Still, I love the place because it is a trendy student type and a music free zone. The more sophisticated clientele of the estate drink in the wine bar across the road or travel on the bus into Liverpool.

The Hundred is in desperate need of a lick of paint and some new furniture, but just like the customers who use it, there is genuine feel about the place that you don't get these days in city pubs

When I arrived after my appointment with Henry Green, I found my partner Shoddy sitting in one of the green armchairs in the snug.

I never classed myself as any good at detective work, and without Shoddy I would probably be working full time as a bouncer in one of the town's many disco bars. I just don't have the sort of brain needed to sort through loads of files or chase contacts to get information. What most people don't realise is that this makes up a good ninety percent of the job. What I do best is the legwork, which I class as the sharp end of our operation.

Shoddy had a pint of beer and a whisky chaser in front of him, and as usual had his nose buried in a magazine. It was amazing, but he fitted in with the dilapidated ambience of The Hundred perfectly.

If you had never had the pleasure of speaking to the guy, you could write him off as nothing more than a drunken bum, and you'd be half right because it is true that he is an alcoholic. He has the look of a vagrant about him and his face, just like the pub, had seen better days. Without a doubt, though, my partner had one of the finest analytical brains of anyone that I have ever met.

When I first met him, he was a senior officer in the Merseyside Police Force. People said that he was destined to become Chief

Constable, but it wasn't to be. Shoddy has a big destructive flaw in his personality, and heroin and alcohol abuse pushed him over the edge, leading him to attempt suicide. He was eventually pensioned off, though there are still a lot of serving police officers that remember just how brilliant he was at the job. Now, he is my eyes, ears, and brain, and as long as I keep him reasonably sober, he is indispensable.

I bought a drink and eased myself into an armchair next to where he was sitting. He ignored me. "What you reading, Shod? I thought you'd be watching the horse racing from Kempton Park."

He looked up. "What's the good of that when you've no money for a bet?"

I nodded. Times had been hard recently."So what is it that's so interesting?"

"Have you ever heard of DNA, Moggs?"

"Isn't that the place in America?"

"What place?"

"You know the one; the place with the White House."

"I think you mean Washington, and that is DC, not DNA."

"What does it stand for?"

"It stands for District of Columbia."

"Not that, you daft bugger. What does DNA stand for?"

He shrugged and drained his whisky. "I'm not sure what the letters mean, but they can use it like fingerprints because everybody has a different one."

"It'll never catch on, mate. Mark my words, nothing is better than fingerprints."

"It says here, Moggs, when DNA takes off, by 2010 they could build a complete human out of it. Imagine that."

I tried to, but I couldn't. "Sorry, Shod, but that's a bit too deep for me; will they also have self-driving cars and pills instead of food?"

"It's not me saying this; it's the magazine. Forensic science is getting very sophisticated; we should move with the times or get left behind."

My partner was in lecture mood. I had to change the subject fast. "I've got us a job, and the client has paid money up front."

"What is he, some kind of an idiot? Get the beers in." Shoddy rubbed his hands in glee. "I can feel a session coming on. Make that doubles."

In a perfect world, I would have given him the list of people and addresses that he needed to check, and left him to get on with it. I had decided to take a look at Ashton's house after the pub, but it never happened. We ended up buying fish and chips at the chip shop on the corner and staggering back to his flat, which was conveniently next door to mine.

I made myself comfortable on the settee and digested my cod and chips. Shoddy made us mugs of thick Yorkshire tea, brought them over and collapsed in his old armchair. He spent so much time in it that there was a permanent indent of his backside on the leather cushion. He rolled himself a cigarette and for the first time mentioned the case we had just taken on.

"So what's it all about, Moggs?"

"It seems straight forward enough. We've got a jealous dad, who is pissed off that his daughter has run off with some American bloke who he doesn't like. He wants me to get some information on him and see if there is any dirt I can dig up. Oh yeah, he also claims that this man in some way is wanted by the police, but can't tell me why.

"It sounds too easy. Can we spin it out to make some more money?"

"The client is loaded, but I don't think he is stupid. I reckon the best thing for me to do is check out where lover boy lives and take it from there." I handed Shoddy a piece of paper with a list of names and addresses. I had added Henry Green at the bottom. It was always a good idea to check out the person who had hired you, to see if they had anything nasty in their past. I had learnt this the hard way.

Shoddy carefully examined the piece of paper. "So I'll get down this list and see what I can find out. When are you going to check out Ashton?"

"Well, it's too late today, and I'm not in a fit state to drive. I'll go first thing tomorrow." I switched on the TV and channel hopped in a vain attempt to find something interesting. There was nothing even remotely watchable, so I switched off and got myself a beer from the fridge. When I got back to my chair, ready to discuss the case some more, Shoddy was fast asleep and snoring.

I made my way to the door and let myself out, vowing to keep well away from the pub at least until I had paid my rent.

CHAPTER THREE

The address that I had for Ashton was in the Wirral, which is a peninsula that forms part of the English border with Wales. North Wales is on the other side of the estuary, though you wouldn't know you were crossing the boundary from England by any physical change.

His house was situated just outside the sleepy village of Barnston, one of the most expensive parts of the zone, which is populated with rich Liverpool shopkeepers and retired gynaecologists and lawyers. Suffice to say they didn't mix that much, down the pub. Most of the houses here have got a Mock-Tudor appeal, and the residents play at being simple village yokels when it suits, but the truth is that the authentic yokels were bought out decades ago when house prices were rock bottom. If Ashton had a place here, then he must be worth a bob or two.

When I stopped my car underneath a sign that said 'The Gables' I couldn't fail to be impressed by the rustic ambience with the underlying feel of cash. The first problem that I encountered, however, was that the actual house was nowhere to be seen. He could be living in a gypsy caravan for all I knew. I needed to get closer. There was an expensive looking iron gate, with a surveillance camera system attached. I noticed that the red brick wall in pristine condition on either side had broken glass cemented into the top, which was always a sure sign that intruders were not welcome.

I opened my glove compartment, got out my powerful German binoculars, drove the Elf into a lay-by further up the road, and began walking around the perimeter of the property. I was looking for an opening that would enable me to get inside the grounds. The wall turned into a hedge, and the hedge eventually provided me with a hole big enough for me to squeeze my six feet four frame through. Even the children of the rich middle-class scrumped for apples and I had noticed the apple and pear orchard a little way back. The hole must have been made by generations of the little blighters even though they could have just asked their rich parents for the money to buy the fruit from the local store. I guess nothing gets the adrenaline going like trespassing, and it was the same for me.

I stumbled my way through the woods, roughly going back in the general direction of where I had parked my car. I hate the countryside and never could understand why people chose to live in it. The torment eventually ended, and I broke out into a huge grass paddock with a couple of horses prancing around and in the distance the chimneys of a grand old regency style house. It wasn't exactly a mansion, but looked authentic, which showed that whatever else he was, Ashton certainly had the taste for the good life.

I found myself an elevated piece of ground and trained my binoculars on the front of the building. Having seen the horses, I was afraid that my next encounter with animals would be a mad pack of Doberman Pinschers or Alsatians. If this man wanted privacy, what better way to keep it than investing in guard dogs? I decided to take a quick look and get out. There was a black Ford Sierra Cosworth parked up alongside a little Renault 5. My luck was in, because as I trained my binoculars on the front door, a man stepped out. Even with glasses, I couldn't distinguish much about him, but I did notice him turn his head and glare in my general direction.

Had he seen the glint off my binoculars in the sunlight? The sun was in the right place. It was time for me to go. He was staring too long for him to be admiring the scenery. Was he hoping to see it again so he could identify where I was? I backed away and found the relative safety of the woods. The last view of the man, who I could only assume was Ashton, was getting into the Renault. As I made my way back to the road, I was relieved that he had chosen French over the powerful Cosworth, because I had every intention of following him, and the little Elf was no match on the open road for the beast that was the Ford.

When I got back to my car, I was sweating with the exertion and just in time to see the gate automatically swing open, and the Renault 5 appear. It drove away sedately, but before I had a chance to turn my car around, a yellow Ford Fiesta appeared at a gap in the hedge across the road from me, swung out of a field and tucked itself in behind. Was I being overly suspicious, or had the car been hidden behind the hedge waiting for Ashton to appear?

The Renault took a right and then a sharp left, and both myself and the Fiesta mimicked it. Ashton was heading into the village, and I wondered if he was aware that he had got a double tail. He pulled into the car park of a pub called the Fox and Hounds and the Fiesta carried on and stopped a little way down the street. I pulled into a space between two cars directly opposite the pub and waited.

The driver of the Fiesta got out. He was a small powerfully built man wearing jeans and a zipped-up bomber jacket. He headed cautiously towards the car park, with a nervous belligerent look on his face. In marked contrast, the driver of the Renault got out of the car in a relaxed manner and stood there waiting. He was an extremely handsome man for his age, with a compact and muscular physique and expensive looking clothing. He had a sort of old James Bond appeal that women go for; I wound down my window so I could catch the action that was obviously going to kick off when the two of them met.

The Fiesta driver looked startled as he turned the corner into the car park and saw Ashton standing there. I am only assuming now that this was Ashton, but I would have laid money on it.

"Are you following me, friend?"

Mr Fiesta tried to bluff it and walk past. Ashton moved over blocking his way. "You were on my property checking out my house with a pair of binoculars before."

"You're mentally disturbed, mate. I don't know what you're on about."

Ashton moved like lightning; he hit Fiesta man hard in the gut and when he bent up double in pain, brought his knee up under his chin. The effect was devastating, and as I watched Ashton get back into his car, I couldn't help but feel sympathy. It had been me with the binoculars, but it was a question of being in the wrong place at the wrong time. I watched as the Renault pulled out of the car park and drove away, and walked over to the man on the floor. He was still groggy, so I took full advantage and pulled his wallet from his inside pocket. The name on his driving licence was Charles Steel. There were a couple of pound notes and a receipt dated yesterday for the Four Bridges Hotel in New Brighton.

Mr Steel seemed to have a fast recovery rate because he snatched the wallet back off me and attempted to get up. I stepped back to give him some space and he rose to his feet shaking his head. "You're a big fucker. Can I have my licence back or are you trying to steal it."

I handed it to him. "Do your friends call you Charles or Charlie?"

"My friends call me Charlie, but I'm Mr Steel to you. What do your friends call you? Shit for Brains?" He made a move to go around me, but I pushed him back, and I could see that he didn't like the contact. As if to confirm this, he swung at me with a left hook that I could have made a cup of tea and still blocked; it was that obvious. I caught his fist and squeezed until I saw the tears in his eyes.

"All right, all right, you daft fucker, let me go." I loosed my grip slowly then released his hand.

"What's your connection with Ashton?"

"Who?"

"The guy that just laid you out, or have you forgotten?"

"Oh, him." He examined me from head to toe. "Are you a cop?"

"That's for me to know, mate. I'll ask you again. What's your connection with Ashton?" I grabbed his jacket and raised my fist, and he seemed to get the message.

"I don't have any connection with him. In fact, this is why I'm here; I'm on what you might call an information gathering exercise. The only thing is, nobody seems to have any information, and from what little time I've been in contact with the guy, he seems to have a mental problem and temper issues." He looked me in the eyes. "It seems like there are a lot of people in this part of the world that could do with some anger management classes." He grinned at me, and I dropped my fist and let him go. He made a play of adjusting his clothing and flashed that wicked grin at me again. "Am I right in saying that I'm not the only party that is interested in Ashton Baxter?"

It was my turn to grin now. "You could say that."

"Well, I think you owe me one for taking a beating when you know it should have been you on the receiving end."

"How do you mean?"

"I saw you going through the hole in the hedge with those friggin binoculars around your neck. I'd been tailing him for a couple of days without any problem at all, and then you came along like a bull in a china shop and screwed it up. Now he knows that he is being followed so is going to be extra careful."

He had got a point. "Yeah, sorry about that Charlie" I handed him a card, and he read it carefully.

"It looks like we are both after the same information, Morris. My cover is well and truly burnt, so I think we need to do a deal. I could make it worth your while to pass anything you get onto me."

"How much worth my while?"

"Let's see what you get first, hotshot."

Where are you staying? I'll see what I can do and contact you."

"You saw my address when you went through my wallet. You can contact me there."

What could I say to that? I had certainly been the reason he had been discovered by Ashton. I stepped aside to let him pass and said I would see him later. If he was excited by the idea, he didn't show it. He got into his car, did a three point turn and accelerated off without giving me a second glance; if I didn't know any better, I would say that this was a very pissed off man.

CHAPTER FOUR

Hazelnut Avenue was a long street that ran between well kept English gardens and huge Georgian houses. I was in Heswall, which was one of the most expensive places to live on Merseyside. There was nothing fake here. These homes were the real deal, and the people that lived in them were cocooned from places like the council estates close by, because of their bank balances.

Henry Green's sister, Verna was taking advantage of the afternoon sun on her particularly massive and manicured lawn. From a distance, she looked like Henry Green in a curly blonde wig. The closer I got the more like his doppelganger she became. She was sitting drinking cocktails with a man that seemed to be disturbed that I was approaching.

He got up finished his drink off and wiped his mouth with a handkerchief that he took from his pocket. He was a small mouse-like young man, with an Ernest Borgnine face and an extreme comb-over hairstyle.

"As you've got company, I'll be on my way, Vee." Without another word, he walked passed me, got into a yellow E-Type Jaguar parked at the side of the house and drove off.

Verna remained sitting at the table and waited for me to get close before speaking. "You're not selling life assurance, are you? If you are, I can tell you that you're wasting your time."

"My name is Morris Shannon; I'm a private detective."

"Does Jenson know you?"

"Jenson?"

"Jenson James, the man that scurried off when he saw you coming. You're not investigating him, are you? I know what solicitors can be like. Even the young ones."

"No, I'm not investigating him, I'm sorry that I disturbed your chat."

"Don't be, it was just boring business, and to be honest, I was looking for an excuse to get rid of him. So if you are not investigating Jenson, is it me under your magnifying glass, Mr Shannon?"

I looked her in the face to see if she was kidding, but there was no trace of a smile. In fact, there was hardly a trace of anything; she looked bored already with our conversation. I was wrong about her being the spitting image of her brother, though. She had the most magnificent sapphire coloured eyed I have had ever seen. She was obviously proud of them because she flashed them like a weapon, and you couldn't help but be impressed. If her face had been less plain looking, she would have been a stunner for her age. I wondered if Jenson was her toy boy.

"So what do you want? Are you going to start following me around and search my home for clues? Don't tell me; a tall, dark stranger was found floating in my pool, and you suspect my butler, Jeeves?"

I didn't reply. I was used to people being embarrassed and talking too much when I told them what job I did. I waited for her to get the jokes off her rather large chest.

"You seem very secretive, Mr Shannon, or are you trying to look seductive. It won't work with me you know. I'm a lesbian and only go for young girls."

This was getting out of hand. "Your brother gave me your address. He is worried about Kristie."

"I see." From where I was standing it didn't look as if she had seen at all. "Well, if it's got something to do with Kristie, then you had better sit down." She pointed me to the metal garden seat that Jenson James had just vacated.

"Is Kristie in some kind of trouble? If she is, I can tell you that it is not like her. She has always been a good girl."

"That's a question that your brother wants answering. He is very worried."

"Henry is always worried, even when he was a toddler he used to worry about his stuffed animals. People don't change, Mr Shannon. Kristie is just another stuffed animal that he has to worry about, especially after he became a single parent. Only, Kristie is anything but, a stuffed toy; she has an active mind and like any young person wants her freedom to make her own way."

"Your brother is not happy with her new boyfriend."

"Yes, I know. He threatened to hire a detective, but I never for a minute thought that he would go through with it. Are you expensive, Mr Shannon?"

I ignored that one. "Mr Green wants me to look into the background of Ashton Baxter to see if there is anything detrimental that could hurt his daughter."

"My! Those are big words, Mr Shannon. Did you think them up as you were on your way here? Unlike my brother, I have formally met Ashton, and I have to say that he was charming, though possibly a little old for her. Perfect for someone like me, though."

"That may well be the case, but about an hour ago, I saw him beat up a man, who he only suspected was following him. Do you think that's the sort of a person that Kristie should be associating with?"

She turned those eyes on me again. "If this man was following him, then he deserved all that he got. Kristie is a beautiful, normal girl who wants some fun in her life. Ashton is mature, good looking, and has enough money for me to know that he is not interested in hers. She deserves a chance at love like anyone else. I do not want my brother or his hired monkey to foul it up." She sighed, reached into her handbag and brought out a chequebook. "If I can't appeal to your morals; how much is Henry paying you? I'll double it."

"I have already got a client."

"I thought your sort worked for the highest bidder."

"My sort, work under contract, and when that contract is finished, my sort find another client."

She tossed the chequebook back into her bag. "Well, in that case, can you try and handle whatever you do with a bit of decorum. In other words, don't mess it up for her. She got up, and I got the impression that I was being dismissed. I took the hint and left.

CHAPTER FIVE

I drove a couple of streets to an address Green had given me, which was supposedly where Kristie's best friend lived. I was still in the posh part of town, and Melinda Spencer-Evan's house was every bit as palatial as Verna's. This time, however, it was a mock Spanish style mansion, which looked as if it needed a lick of paint.

The woman, who answered the door after I had been ringing the bell for a good five minutes, was dressed like a cleaning lady in a dirty old grey pinny with a crimson scarf tied around her head like a pirate.

"Don't they have bells where you come from?"

"How do you mean?"

"You seemed to be having fun playing with ours. I heard you the first time, Luv."

"So how come it took you so long to answer?"

She looked me up and down in an attempt to make me feel belittled and wiped her hands on a dirty old towel. "We don't want insurance, and we have already got double-glazing."

"I'm not selling anything; I want to speak to Melinda. Is that possible?"

"Anything's possible; I'll see if she is up yet." She turned around and kicked the door closed in my face. I looked at my watch. It was two o'clock. How could she still be in bed? People in Heswall weren't noted for their manners, but even by their low standards, the people I had spoken to today were pretty grim. I hoped that Melinda was going to be an exception, though, with a surname like Spencer-Evans, I wasn't counting on it.

I was just about to give up and head to the pub for a late lunch when the cleaning lady appeared again at the door. She said that Melinda would see me, and I followed her into an oak-panelled study with a bay window overlooking a huge garden with a lily pond in the middle. Very picturesque!

More waiting, but at last, the door opened and in stumbled the girl herself. She had long dark hair an unhealthy white face and a chin and teeth that reminded me of a horse. She looked like she had just got up and hadn't had a coffee yet.

She walked around me without acknowledging I was in the room, vaguely waved me to sit down and dropped onto the settee like she was about to pass out. Up close her skin was so white it was almost transparent. I wondered how much blood she had spilling around inside her. She examined me with pinned out sleepy dark eyes as if she was challenging me to accuse her of substance abuse. I wasn't going to, in my head, it was cut and dried that she was a druggy. What did I care? How she treated her body was no concern of mine; I watched her watching me, watching her and waited for her to deliver something profound.

"You're that detective person that Kristie's dad hired," she said in a triumphant voice.

I wasn't expecting that. "How come you know, Melinda?"

"Because he telephoned me and said that you might call around to ask me a few questions. He said you were a huge brute of a man with a bald head, and I was to tell you what I know."

"And what do you know?"

"I know lots of things. It depends on what you want to hear."

"Well, for a start, what do you think about Ashton Baxter?"

"The jury is still out on Ashton. There are some people, mainly girls, that think the sun shines from his backside, and there are others that think he's an old bullshitter."

"And you? What do you think?"

"He's American, and a bit old. Some girls go for older men, but combined with being a Yank is just too much. They are such a loud lot over there. They aren't particularly civilised in that part of the world. They should never have had that party in Boston."

"Oh yeah, which party was that?"

She looked at me as if I was brain damaged and moved on. "He is rich, and he does like throwing it around."

"Do you think that he is interested in Kristie because she has money?"

"Have you met Kristie yet?"

"No, I haven't had the pleasure."

"Well let me tell you, she doesn't need to have money to get any man she wants. Whenever we used to go out, she was the one that the good looking guys went for. I just tagged on to her designer coattails and picked up the scraps. But even the scraps that Kristie didn't want were often out of my league."

"What happened to Kristie's mum?"

"I only know what I've heard, didn't Mr Green tell you?"

"I'd like another angle. What happened to her, Melinda?"

"She killed herself."

Why?"

Melinda shrugged. "Who knows, she always seemed happy enough, then one day she hangs herself. Kristie was devastated.

Well, we all were at the time, but Kristie never got over it. She seemed to change somehow; became more distant, less friendly."

"But there was no reason that you know of why she would have done it?"

"Hell no, I was just a teenager at the time, why would anybody tell me. You're the detective; even I can see that the person you want to ask is Kristie's dad. He's a big softy. He let the mum run rings around him."

Talk to Kristie's dad. I couldn't argue with the logic in that. I gave her a card, thanked her for seeing me and left.

CHAPTER SIX

I popped into the office on the way back to my flat and saw that the red light of my answer phone was flashing, meaning that I had a message. It was Henry Green asking if I would phone him back. I dialled the number, and Green picked it up on the second tone. He sounded as if he had been running or maybe he was practising his heavy breathing telephone technique.

"I saw him in the club today, Shannon. Bold as brass playing 18 holes with one of the golf pros."

I assumed he was talking about Ashton. "I thought membership was exclusive."

"He must have got himself a sponsor for the day. Can you come now and have dinner with me? Maybe you can get talking to him and see what his intentions are."

"You're not thinking of hitting him again are you, Mr Green?"

"I don't want anything to do with him. Come for dinner; we can discuss what you are doing for the money I am paying you."

It sounded like a direct order, and who was I to argue with a rich client. I said that I would be there for eight o'clock and made my way to Shoddy's place. At least dinner at the golf club restaurant would beat meat pie and chips from the chip shop.

Out of all the people on the list that I had given to my partner earlier, he had come up with exactly zero information. He assured me that there were things going on behind the scenes that could lead to him having something in his hand the next day, but I wasn't going to hold my breath. I scraped off my old shirt and put on a new one with a cleaner tie. I sponged the curry stains off my suit jacket, grabbed my car keys and headed off for my appointment.

The man at the reception desk informed me the restaurant was not open until eight o'clock and that Mr Green was still playing golf. I looked at my watch, I was half an hour early, I went through to the bar where I had first met him and ordered a drink. At the far side of the room was a door marked 'Changing.' I was halfway through a beer when who should come out but Ashton Baxter with some man I had never seen before. Ashton headed off towards the reception area but the man, who was dressed in typical golfing gear, came over to

51

the bar and ordered a tomato juice. He sat perkily on the bar stool next to me and nursed his drink. He was in his mid-twenties with a muscular physique and blond hair that was cut short. He had the air about him of somebody with nowhere to go, so when he knocked the tomato juice back in one, I moved in on him, hoping that he didn't think I was trying to pick him up.

"Do you want another one?"

He handed his glass back to the bartender and said, "Yeah, why not," without even looking at me. If he was the golf pro that Ashton had been playing with, I suppose he was used to members hitting on him, in the hope of some free advice on how to improve their swing.

"I guess playing golf every day keeps you pretty fit."

He instinctively looked down at his huge pectorals, with a look of pride on his face. "I also do a lot of work in the gym. Golf is ninety percent technique, so you don't need to be muscle bound, but I get more work from the ladies if I look good." He laughed to himself as if this was a private joke between him and his ego, and continued nursing his drink.

"So how many golf pros are there in the club?"

"Too many to make any real money."

"Isn't America where the top money is for golf pros?"

"Yes, you're right. I was just talking to an American who told me the same thing."

"Do you mean Ashton Baxter?"

He looked at me for the first time since he had sat down. "I've just done 18 holes with him. Do you know him?"

"Let's just say I know of him. He's from Washington isn't he?"

"New York."

"That's right; he's from New York, I Remember now. So is he any good?"

"He didn't embarrass himself."

I had to think fast to squeeze the guy for information. I was lucky that he didn't seem too intelligent. "I didn't know he was a member of this club. I thought he was too busy working. I can't remember what line of business he is in; was it clothes shops?"

He seemed to find this amusing. "No. You must be thinking of another Ashton Baxter. He told me that he was an entrepreneur."

I whistled. "Entrepreneur eh? What's one of those?"

"I think that they buy and sell things, but he never went into that."

"So who signed him into the club?"

"That would have been Mrs Gibbs. She came in this morning and did the paperwork."

"Is that Henry Green's sister?"

"Do you know Mr Green?" I nodded, and he lowered his voice and leaned over. "Well, don't tell him that she did that because he and Ashton Baxter don't get on. Everybody knows in the club, and whenever Mr Baxter plays we are all a bit tense in case they meet."

"So Ashton has played here before then."

"Not with me, but he does come down occasionally to play a round."

I signalled to the barman to get us both refills. "You've got me intrigued. What is the argument about?"

"The whisper is that the two of them were arguing in a hotel somewhere, and Mr Green threw a punch and was arrested by the police. Don't say that I said anything, though."

"So what was it about?"

The fight was over Kristie Green, Mr Green's daughter."

Before I had a chance to question him more, the receptionist popped her head around the door and called him. He thanked me for the drink and trudged away.

Green still hadn't showed and with the prices they were charging at the bar, I couldn't afford anything else, so I decided to do a bit of exploring. I wandered aimlessly around outside and eventually found what I was looking for. There was a small driving range with three mats and buckets containing balls. Ashton was on the middle one, and I watched as he struck a ball high and straight into the night air.

"Good shot," I said, and he turned around and examined me.

He had a good looking intense sort of a face with dark, broody eyes. He looked me in the face for a couple of seconds as if he was computing whether we had met before. His filing system must have come up blank because he turned away and went over to the bucket to get another ball.

"Do you know where I can go to book one of the mats?"

"No"

I couldn't get a fix on the accent with just the one word. "Sorry, let me put that question another way. How did you book a mat?"

He placed the ball carefully on the tee. Did a couple of practice runs then swung perfectly and connected. He didn't even watch the flight but turned to face me again. "I didn't book anything; I just took out my driver and started to practice."

"So it's free then."

"Yes, it is."

"Are you American?"

"Why, is there a law against it?"

"No, it's just that we don't see many Americans in this part of the world."

"Have you got a problem with Americans, friend?"

This was one aggressive character. "I haven't got a problem with anybody; I was just asking for information."

He reached into the bucket again and picked out a ball. "Well, now you've got it."

I watched him place the ball on the tee and go through his practice swing again. He had jet black hair and a Roman nose. He was probably in his late fifties and definitely didn't like making polite conversation. I got the hint and went back to the bar. Henry Green was sitting at the same table where I had met him previously. His hair was wet and his face shiny and red. When he saw me, he put his hand in the air like a mixed infant in a maths lesson. I half expected him to snap his fingers again. Green was the sort of person who was used to instant service and expected results and fast for the money he was paying out. I walked over, leisurely and sat down.

CHAPTER SEVEN

Green looked as if he hadn't slept for a week. He stood up as I approached as if he was eager to start eating. It was a buffet, and he led me over to a long trestle table and told me to help myself to food and drink. I followed behind him as he proceeded to fill his plate with as much food as it would hold. I tried to be good and not make a pig of myself and just took some roast chicken and a potato salad.

When we sat down, he ordered wine, but when he saw the look on my face also ordered a pitcher of beer as well. Talking to him while he was gorging himself was impossible, and by the time he had finished the food on his first plate, and gone back to the trestle table for seconds, almost an hour had passed us by. I declined desert and watched him demolish a huge slice of carrot cake and finish off with Irish coffee. We had eaten in virtual silence. I waited for him to drain his coffee and tossed him a question to digest along with the food. "So tell me, Mr Green. Does Kristie have much experience with men?"

He looked at me for a couple of seconds as if the meal had wiped out the fact that I was sitting at the table. He cleaned his mouth with a napkin and threw it down on the plate in front of him."She never brought any boyfriends home, if that's what you mean. She had a lot of girlfriends, but she tended to keep herself to herself when it came to boys."

"Or maybe she was secretive."

"Kristie is not a devious kind of person, if you knew her, then you would understand what I mean. She had friends of both sexes; she just didn't get seriously involved with any of them."

"Until now."

"Until now," he repeated under his breath.

"So where did she meet Ashton Baxter?"

"I haven't got a clue, Shannon. He just appeared. One minute he wasn't on the scene and the next he was."

"You said before that you thought the death of her mother could have made her more vulnerable."

"Like I said; she was very close to her mother. Maybe she was looking for affection and Ashton was in the right place at the right time."

"But you don't believe that do you, Mr Green? Why do you really think she fell for Ashton, and why are you so set against him?"

"I tell you, Shannon, the man is scum and that he is dangerous. All I want you to do is to prove it, and if you don't think you are up to the job, I am going to have to find somebody who will. Now, I asked you to come here not for me to answer damn silly questions, which I have already given you the answers to. I asked you to come here to give me your report on what you have found out so far. You seem to have forgotten who the employer is and who is being employed."

"Yes, thanks for reminding me that was silly of me. So far I have not found out anything of any relevance, and I need more time. I do happen to think that the death of her mother could have had implications, but if you are not prepared to give me the details, then I am going to have to find out for myself."

"Her mother was depressed. She was on strong medication and spent more time in hospital and lying on couches talking to shrinks than she did at home. We have a holiday home in Trearddur Bay; she went there on her own one weekend and hung herself from a wooden beam. I suppose the depression got too much for her, and she couldn't take anymore."

Talking about his wife seemed to have depressed him. He played around with the sugar lumps in the bowl with his teaspoon. Finally, he looked me in the face. "Mr Shannon, is it possible for you to put all of your efforts into turning up something on Ashton. He could be married for instance, or could he be a criminal. I'm expecting you to find something. Is it more money that you want for a result?"

This man was desperate. "If there is nothing to turn up, then no matter how much money you pay me, I am not going to find anything." That deflated him so much that he got up and headed for the trestle table. He returned with another plate full of food; he simply said, "I won't keep you from your work, Mr Shannon." I was being dismissed in disgrace. He put his arm around the plate while he was eating as if to protect the food on it. I knew when I wasn't wanted. I got up thanked him for the meal and left.

As I made my way to my car, a figure stepped out of the shadows and blocked my path. "Mr Shannon?

She was an attractive blonde, which by the look of her expensive coat and makeup, wasn't short of money.

"Do I know you," I asked.

"You don't know me personally, Mr Shannon, but you have been asking a lot of questions about me."

The penny dropped. I held my hand out, which she ignored. "You're Kristie Green?"

"This is a small place and word gets around. I am assuming that my dad is paying you money to dig up information on Ashton. Is that correct?"

"I think you should talk to your father about that, Miss Green. He is in the restaurant now. Why don't you go in and clear the air?"

"Clearing any air between my father and I is not your concern. If you have any questions why not ask me?" She added, "I love Ashton with all my heart, and I know that he feels the same."

"I think that your father is just a little concerned about the length of time you have known him and the age difference."

"Do you believe in love at first sight, Mr Shannon?"

"Er, I'm not qualified to answer this, Miss. All I can say is that your dad is only thinking of you."

"So what do you want to know about Ashton?"

"Your dad wants to know; he just hired me to ask the questions. So where did you meet him?"

"We met in New York. I was on a trip with my aunt, Verna. That was months ago. He wants us to get married. And no; don't even think that he is after my money because he has got much more than I have."

"So what does he do to get his money?"

"He is a business man."

" That covers a lot of ground, Miss Green. What sort of business?"

"Stuff that I don't understand. He tried to explain a couple of times, but it's just a boring load of old figures to me. When we get married, he wants us to go and live in America, so you can tell my dad that I will be out of his hair for good soon unless he apologises to Ashton and me for being such a horrible old man."

She reminded me of a female version of Bambi, and I could see why her father was worried. I had only met her for a couple of minutes, and even I wanted to put my arm around her and protect her from the big bad American. "With all due respect, I spoke to Ashton a couple of hours ago, and my first impression was that he didn't look the sort of man that wanted to settle down," As the words left my mouth I realised that they should have remained as thought in my head. Tears began to run down her face. I pulled out a handkerchief from my pocket, realised that I had blown my nose on it earlier, and stuffed it back."

"You're a nasty man just like my dad. How could you say such a thing? Ashton is very loving....................."

"What's going on here?" A man forcibly pushed me out of the way and put his arm around Kristie. It was Ashton. He must have been on his way home. He gripped me with a steely stare, daring me to give him an excuse so he could hit me.

"So who the hell are you, buddy? Do you enjoy making women cry?"

"Yeah, it's a hobby of mine." Somehow I didn't think backing down to Ashton Baxter would have been a good idea. I was using attack as the best means of defence. When it came to sarcasm, I am unbeatable.

Kristie hid her face in his chest, and in the awkward silence between us, I could almost hear his brain cells whirling around, wondering if he should punch me. I reckon that if he had thought he could have taken me, he would have done. As it was, my height must have saved me from a pounding.

He tried to save face as he led Kristie away. "Don't let me catch you hanging around me or my girl again, otherwise you are dead. Capisce?"

I understood alright, but I wasn't convinced that his intentions with Kristie Green were honourable. It had been a long day, and I was tired of the lot of them. I fired up the Elf and headed home.

CHAPTER EIGHT

"This bacon tastes a bit off to me, Shod."

We were having breakfast in Shoddy's flat, and I was trying to milk him for information about the list of people I had given him. He walked over picked up my plate and smelt the bacon. "It seems alright to me. Anyway, it's not going to give you food poisoning." He added "I hope," as he walked over to the kitchen area and finished off pouring the tea.

I'd gone through the events of the day before while he was frying up the breakfast, but I wasn't sure if he was taking it all in. I suspected that he had been drunk the previous night and had woken up with a big hangover. I hoped that the bacon, eggs, sausage, tomatoes, black pudding and toast would put a lining of grease on his stomach and sober him up. There was nothing like a big English breakfast to snap the fuzziness out of your head after a bellyful of beer. It was like having a bucket of ice water thrown over you. I buttered a piece of toast and spread thick orange marmalade over it.

"You haven't told me what you've got. Did you come up with anything?"

He brought the tea over, lit up a cigarette and finished off the last piece of sausage on his plate.

"I had to pull in a few favours down at the police station for information on Ashton Baxter. There is nothing on him in Britain, but as he is American, it's going to take some time."

"How long?"

"A couple of days, maybe more. It's difficult to say."

"What about Kristie Green?"

"Clean as a whistle. I even got her final year exam results, and she is pure as the driven snow. Except....."

"Except what?"

"Well, you know what happened to her mother."

"Yeah, she killed herself."

"It's not quite as simple as that. Because the family house is just outside Croxley, they sent some detectives up to North Wales to help the local lads. Our old friend DCI Jenkins led the investigation."

"That bag of shite. So what did he conclude?"

"I got to look at the case notes, but I had to buy my mate in the records department a few drinks for the privilege. That's why I am so hung over this morning."

"My heart bleeds for you, Shod."

"I couldn't let him drink on his own, it wouldn't have been sociable, and besides we talked about the case until he was too drunk to put coherent sentences together."

"So what's the problem?"

"The problem is that even though she hung herself, there was a definite feeling that she had been helped if you know what I mean."

"Helped in what way?"

"They found her hanging from a wooden beam, and it looked as if she had climbed onto a coffee table and then kicked it away. But, there were signs on her wrists that she had been tied up."

"So she was murdered, and it was made to look like suicide."

"I never said that. I said that she had been tied and then put into a noose."

"That's what I meant; she was murdered."

Shoddy took a long drink of his tea. "There was no sign of a struggle; she was dressed in a leather basque with black fishnet stockings and she'd had sex just before she died. What does that say to you, Moggs?"

"It doesn't say anything, mate. Was she murdered or not?"

"The general feeling by the lads investigating the case at the time was that she had willingly been tied up and had willingly submitted to the noose being put around her neck."

"Why would she do that?"

"Some women enjoy being choked while having sex. Once the oxygen is cut off to the brain, you get up to ten seconds before passing out. More if you are expert at it. During this moment your sexual pleasure will go through the roof. It is supposed to be the ultimate orgasm. Some women even enjoy being choked unconscious, but let's say that these are advanced users. Jenkins couldn't prove it, but he thought that Kristie Green's mother had been tied up and then hung from the ceiling while having sex."

"So there was somebody else there with her."

Shoddy looked at me as if I was an idiot. "That was the conclusion. Now, whether it was a perverted act of sexual pleasure that went horribly wrong, or it was murder after having sex; nobody could say. Either way, she died from asphyxiation."

"Did it all come out in the autopsy?"

"Not in that way. As far as the coroner was concerned, she hung herself. The fact that she'd had sex beforehand was not considered relevant, except that the husband told police that it wasn't with him."

"Any more tea, Shod?"

He got up took my mug and filled it up from the teapot. "There are a few curious side issues that I also found out. Green's wife had all the money, and he was virtually penniless."

"He didn't look poor to me."

"She made her money in the sex industry. She had some sex shops in Merseyside and Manchester, and she sold out and made a fortune. She was loaded. Henry Green worked in the local council offices before they met, as a draughtsman?"

"He looked like a pen-pusher."

"His wife was far smarter than he was, and also made sure that her daughter would be looked after financially if she died. She set up a trust fund, and it all went to Kristie. Whatever the father gets is due to her good nature. She didn't leave him anything."

"So Kristie keeps the dad in food and drink."

"She also pays the mortgage on the house and one other thing."

"I'm all ears, Shod, you have been busy."

"Kristie is not his daughter. He didn't even adopt her after he married the mother."

"So who is the real father?"

"I don't know that, but it is not Henry that's for sure."

"That seems like a very good reason why Henry Green wants me to dig up the dirt on Ashton. If she leaves and gets married, what's to stop her cancelling his income from the trust fund? Like you said, she's not his daughter."

"How do they get on, Moggs?"

"I've never seen them in the same room together so I couldn't say. Green is trying to play the protective father, who is outraged that she has got mixed up with a villain, but when I met her, she didn't say one way or another, what their relationship was like. All she said was for me to stop asking questions about her."

"So where do we go from here?"

"Well, I'm going back out to Ashton's place to have a nose around. If you can find out anything about his activities in America, it would be helpful. Kristie told me that he was a businessman."

"She could be right."

"She could be, but no business man I know could lay somebody out cold like I saw Ashton do yesterday. He is extremely fit for his age. He looks and acts like a professional criminal, so it's just possible that Green's concerns are justified."

"And what about Kristie? What's she like as a person?"

"She doesn't come across as very worldly, to be honest. If I was going to rip somebody off, then she looks ideal."

"But what would be the reason if Ashton has got money?"

"It could all be for show. Houses can be rented and not paid for and so can flash cars. He could be scamming her out of her inheritance. For all we know, Green could be right. Maybe he has done this before, and that's why he has got money. There are too many questions and hardly any answers at the moment, mate."

"So, you are off to Ashton's house?"

"Can you think of anywhere better for me to go? If I'm there, I can at least follow him discreetly.

Shoddy picked up the plates and mugs and took them over to the sink. I grabbed my hat and coat and made my way to the door. It was ten o'clock, and I was ready for anything, which is just as well, the way the next 24 hours panned out.

CHAPTER NINE

The drive to Ashton's house in Barnston should have taken me less than an hour, even in the Elf with its limited acceleration. By the time I was halfway there, I was seriously thinking about handing in my final report to Green and telling him that there was nothing more I could do. What Shoddy had told me about his financial reliance on Kristie, pointed to the fact that he was just scared that she was going to cut him off.

I was driving on autopilot, and as I swept through a small wood about a mile from the village, my mind was so focused on the case I almost missed the yellow Fiesta in the lay-by. I braked, backed up, then pulled in and parked directly behind it. I don't think I had ever seen a yellow Fiesta before, so I was certain that it belonged to Charlie Steel.

The car wasn't locked, and the key was in the ignition. I put my hand on the bonnet, and it was cold. I looked around me. This was a particularly isolated place, and no cars had passed since I had left my vehicle. On either side of the road, there was a thick hawthorn hedge behind which stood a wooded area that looked about as inviting as an open grave. This would not be a place that I would have chosen to spend the night. Even in daylight, it was easy to imagine all sorts of horrors lurking in the shadows. I wondered if Charlie was hiding in the trees watching me. It was then that I saw the blood on the steering wheel, and the odds of that were slashed. This didn't look good.

Behind the hedge, on my side of the road, I heard a loud crack like somebody had snapped a branch. I went over to the hedge stood on tiptoes and peered over. In the clearing where the wood ended, there was a man in orange overalls loading logs onto a trailer at the back of a tractor. He reached over picked up an axe and started to chop at some thick branches lying on the ground. I could see that there was also a chainsaw at his feet for the bigger pieces. I walked a bit further down the road until I came to a gate and climbed over.

The man was so involved in his work that he didn't notice me approaching, even though I had subtly coughed as I didn't want to give him a fright while he was holding an axe. Finally, after I had feigned a coughing fit, he turned around, saw me and walked in my direction. He tossed the axe onto the trailer before he started to walk, which was a relief.

"This is private property. Didn't you see the sign on the gate?"

"I just want some information. I'm looking for a friend of mine."

"I ain't seen nobody all day, pal, just you."

"That's his car over there, the yellow Fiesta. He's a smallish man and is possibly wearing jeans and a bomber jacket. Are you sure that you haven't seen him?"

"That's what I said didn't I?"

He was within touching distance now, and I could smell his body odour and bad breath. He was a huge beast of a man that probably had issues with anger management if that fiery look in his eyes was anything to go by. Maybe it was him that had attacked Charlie. He had an axe and a chainsaw.

"What about the car? Was it here when you started work this morning?"

"It was here when I started work yesterday. I think your friend must have abandoned it."

"Are you sure you haven't seen the driver?"

He didn't give me the courtesy of an answer to my question. He turned and walked away lifted his arm up in a mocking goodbye gesture and shouted over his shoulder. "Like I said, mate; this is private property."

Meeting over: I never did like these country types. They seemed to have been interbred and shared a very limited intelligence and volcanic tempers. I obviously couldn't walk into the woods to have a look around; otherwise, the workman could well have run after me with his axe or chainsaw. I remembered that Charlie had said he was staying in the Four Bridges Hotel in New Brighton. Maybe he had run out of petrol and bummed a lift back, or maybe pigs could fly. I walked over to the Fiesta and turned the key. The engine burst into life first time so that theory was wrong. I climbed back into the Elf, did a three-point turn and headed for New Brighton.

CHAPTER TEN

The Four Bridges Hotel is on the A554 just before New Brighton. The reception area was in need of more than just a lick of paint, and the furniture was a dusty collection that looked like it had come from a house clearance sale in a low-class neighbourhood. The TV was on, but there was nobody sitting down watching it, which didn't surprise me. The hotel like the seaside town of New Brighton that it served was long past its best if it ever had a best. This was the sort of establishment that the local hookers probably rented rooms by the hour.

I took advantage of an empty reception desk to quickly look at the register. I found Charlie Steel as the last entry, so business couldn't be that good. The room number was 35. I scanned the pigeonholes behind the desk and couldn't see a key for that number. It was looking optimistic. I rang the bell, and a seedy looking unshaven man appeared in an off white vest.

He gave me the faint promise of a smile, turned the register around and snapped it shut.

"Do you want a room?"

"It's possible. Is Charlie Steel in?"

"I haven't seen him today."

"He's in 35, isn't he? I noticed that the key is not behind the desk."

He gave me a strange look. "They took two rooms, 35 and 37. I think his sister must have taken 35. It's en-suite," he said with pride.

"Is it possible to speak to his sister? Maybe she could tell me where I could get in touch with Mr Steel."

"You can try, but I don't think she knows herself. He hasn't been here for a couple of days. She asked me this morning if I'd seen him. She didn't look that concerned when I said no. Still, it takes all sorts I say. You certainly see life when you own a hotel. Are you a cop?"

I showed him my ID. "I'm a private investigator. Why do you ask?"

"In this business, you get a smell for trouble, and he looked like trouble. She's alright; a real lady. You know what? I don't even think that he is her brother."

"So what do you think?"

He shrugged. "What do I care? As long as they pay me, they can do what they like. Do you want me to call her on the house phone?"

I was surprised that he had a house phone. "No, you're OK; I'll go up and knock on the door. Room 35 you say?"

He nodded and disappeared into the back, mumbling to himself.

There was no lift, so I made my way up the stairs. Room 35 was at the end of a shabby corridor. I listened at the door before knocking. Whoever was in there was listening to afternoon television. As soon as I knocked, it went quiet inside.

A woman's voice said, "Who is it?"

"Room service."

She opened the door and was about to speak, but I walked into the room before she had a chance. I shut the door behind me and got ready to put my hand over her mouth if she screamed. She didn't. She just stared and waited for me to say something. I handed her my ID, and she read it and handed it back.

"Is this anything to do with Charlie?" She asked

"I'm looking for Charlie Steel if that's what you mean."

"He's dead isn't he?"

"I don't know. You tell me. Why do you think that?"

"Because I haven't seen him for two days, and when he left he said that he would only be a couple of hours."

She walked over to the bedside table took out a cigarette from a carton and lit it. She seemed to have relaxed. The ID has that effect on people.

"So what's your interest in finding Charlie?"

"Let's just say, Miss.....?

"Mrs..."

"Let's just say that Charlie and I share a common interest in the same person."

She didn't look convinced. She gave me the impression that she had stopped trusting people a long time ago. She was dressed in an expensive style that showed off the best parts of her figure and hid the worse. The clothes combined with her tanned skin and high-class English accent led me to deduce that this was somebody used to having money that had fallen on hard times.

"What's the real reason that you are here, Mr Shannon?"

"Like I said before, Charlie and I share a common interest and now that he has gone missing, I am a little bit concerned for his health."

"So why are you so concerned?"

"Because what happened to him might happen to me; I believe in getting to the bottom of mysteries, and at this moment in time, the whereabouts of Charlie is top of my list, Mrs......?"

I was waiting for her to fill in the silence, and grudgingly she obliged. "It's Page, Nina Page, if you must know." Giving me the information about her name seemed to drain the aggression out of her. She went over to the wardrobe and brought out a bottle of gin and two glasses. "Do you want one?"

I hate gin. "Yeah, just a small one."

She poured out half a glass and handed it to me. "I'm sorry, but I've run out of tonic, and the hotel doesn't sell it."

She sat on the edge of the double bed, and I pulled up a chair from under the desk and waited for the story that I knew was coming. I didn't say anything as I wanted her to collect her thoughts.

"When you said that you had a common interest with Charlie, I assume that you meant Harper. Am I right?"

"Harper? Who is he?"

"You probably know him as Ashton Baxter, but I believe that he has numerous aliases."

"I do know an Ashton Baxter, and that is how I came to meet Charlie. He said he was investigating him. What's your connection in this?"

"It's a long story, Mr Shannon."

"I've got all day, and please call me Morris."

"Well, Morris, my husband was a good provider, and when I married him, I knew that the money we had was not earned from what you would call normal labour."

"You mean he was a thief."

"He wasn't a common thief; he was a confidence trickster."

"A grifter?"

"If you like. But anyway my husband, Rudi worked on his own for many years and was always a good provider and never spent any time in prison. He was good at what he did, Morris. And then....."

She poured more gin into my glass and filled up hers. The suspense was killing me. "So what happened?"

"He only mentioned it just the once. He told me he was working with somebody called Harper, and they had set up a blackmail scam, which was going to make them a lot of money. Rudi went to Paris and said he would be back in a couple of weeks. I never usually heard from him while he was working, so I wasn't worried until a month went by and still no message."

"What happened?"

"What happened, Morris was that I hired Charlie Steel to go to Paris to look for him after I tried to use my credit card and found out there was no money in the account. Charlie eventually discovered that Rudy had been poisoned and was dead, and I had realised by then that all of our accounts had been cleaned out of money. To put it bluntly, Morris, I had lost my husband and all of our money. I had to sell my jewellery just to get by. His partner, Harper, was nowhere to be seen, and I kept Charlie on to find him and get my money back. Obviously, I couldn't go to the police."

"So how are you so certain it was Harper that did this to you?"

"It had to be. Who else could have done it?"

"So what has Charlie found out?"

"We know that Harper was just one of the many names used by my husband's ex-partner. We have been on the trail now for over eighteen months. We started off in New York. It was there that Charlie linked up the name Harper with Ashton Baxter, and we followed the trail here. Something big is about to happen, and when it does, I want to be there to fuck it up for him and get my money back."

"So much for honour amongst thieves," I said.

"There is nothing honourable about Ashton Baxter. Charlie has pretty much checked out his criminal credentials, and they go from ripping off just about anybody, including gullible young ladies.

"Ah, I see; you mean the Kristie Green connection."

She went into the drawer of the bedside table, pulled out a file and passed it to me. "You'll find everything in there. One good thing about Charlie is that he writes everything down. That file is up to date up to the time he went missing."

"Can I keep it to read later?"

"Help yourself. Without him, it's no use to me." She examined my face and hit me with a direct question. "Do you think something has happened to him?"

"There is that possibility. I found his car with the keys in."

This seemed to bring her to life. She jerked upright in her seat. "Why didn't you tell me that before?"

"It slipped my mind."

Now she began to get nervous. "Who the hell are you?"

"I told you, my name is Morris Shannon, and I'm working for a client who is investigating our mutual friend Ashton Baxter."

"You sure you're not working for Baxter?" she picked up the gin bottle and held it in front of her like it was a club. "I think you had better go before I start screaming."

That suited me fine. I think I had got as much as I could talking to her, and the file would hopefully make some interesting reading. I threw my card on the bed and left. I wondered how long it would be before she did the same, but I couldn't be bothered waiting outside

to follow her. She wasn't going to lead me anywhere interesting.

CHAPTER ELEVEN

On the off chance, I drove past Henry Green's sister Verna's house. More for something to do than anything else, I parked up and knocked the door. I was particularly interested in her opinion about the suicide of her brother's wife. Maybe she could enlighten me on the family's verdict. It was at least five minutes before I got an answer, and when the door was eventually opened it was Jenson James who stood in the hall eying me suspiciously. That was the second time in two visits that I had met him here. He looked as if had dressed in a bit of a hurry; I wondered if he was married and if his wife would approve.

"What do you want?" I like a man who is direct.

"My name is Shannon; Mo........"

"I know who you are, what I don't know is what you are doing here at this time of the day."

I looked at my watch. It was four o'clock. "Is there any chance that I could have a quick word with Mrs Gibbs?"

"She's not available at the moment, come back tomorrow at a more reasonable hour."

"How about I talk to you if she's not able to make it? Mrs Gibbs told me that you are a solicitor, does that mean you are the family solicitor?"

"I don't think that my position with the Green family is any business of yours?"

"I have been hired by Henry Green to investigate Kristie Green's new man friend, did you know?"

"I am not interested in what Henry gets up to. Investigating a case sounds rather grand. Are you sure that you're not barking up the wrong tree? They looked a very happy couple to me the last time I saw them together. I haven't seen Kristie more radiant."

"Who is it, Jenson?"

Verna Gibbs came down the stairs into the hall. She looked as if she had just grabbed the nearest dress and pulled it over her head. When she saw me, she went into welcome mode and switched on an icy smile. "Come in Mr Shannon. What can I do for you? Let him in, Jenson, where are you manners?"

Jenson's expression went through several changes from temper tantrum to indifferent acceptance. He picked up his car keys from a table near the door and passed me on the way out. "I'll ring you tomorrow, Vee. He didn't acknowledge my presence as he closed the door, but I couldn't say that it bothered me.

I followed Verna into the expensively furnished lounge and took a seat. She sat down opposite. "You'll have to excuse Jenson, Mr Shannon; he can be a bit aggressive in his mannerisms.

I was waiting for her to continue and tell me that underneath he had a heart of gold, but she left it at that. "I'm sorry to disturb you, but I've come up with a few questions that I hope you can help me with."

"Peter's still worried about Kristie, then?"

"I take it that you don't get on well with you brother?"

"We have our ups and downs. Let's just say that Kristie and Ashton is one of our downs. He blames me that they met, but it was fate."

"How do you mean fate?"

"I promised to take Kristie on a trip and told her to choose the place. She chose New York, and that's where she met Ashton. Peter blames me for taking her, but she could have gone on her own anyway, and probably would have. She is a financially independent lady and can go where she pleases. In fact, Mr Shannon, she often does."

"So how did they meet?"

"At a party, I think or was it in one of those awful single bars that they have out there. I really can't remember how it happened or who picked who up. She tended to do her own thing at night, and I tended to relax in the hotel bar. Of course, Peter will not get it out of his head that it was all because she came to live with me, but who could blame the girl. She is in her twenties, and he was still treating her like she was a child."

"I believe that she is not his daughter. Is that right?"

"What are you implying?"

"I'm not implying anything, but it's true that she is not his daughter, isn't it?"

"No, Henry is not her real father, but I hardly think that this has anything to do with the reason she left home and came to live with me. She felt as if she was a prisoner with him. He is too over protective, especially after Mary tragically died."

"Mary was Mr Green's wife? Right!"

She nodded.

"What is your opinion about the suicide?"

"How do you mean opinion? It is cut and dried; she got depressed and killed herself."

"So there was no foul play suspected?"

"No. Wherever did you get that idea from?"

"How would you describe your sister in law, Mrs Gibbs?"

Her eyes widened and looked as though somebody had just flicked a light switch on inside her head. "You are talking about the sex shops and the way she made her money. Just because she made a lot of money selling outrageous clothing and sex aids, didn't mean that she was into perversion. I heard talk about what they thought she was doing at the time of her death, but that was nonsense. If you knew Mary, then you would have laughed at the idea. She had a few shops very much like the Ann Summers sexy lingerie chain. She did parties in people's houses and worked hard to build up her brand. That didn't mean that she was a sex maniac. Far from it; she was just a business woman who was good at her job."

"So why did she kill herself."

"Don't you think I've asked myself that? I don't know, and Henry was devastated."

"She never left him anything."

"My, you have done your homework, Mr Shannon. No, she didn't leave him anything; it all went to Kristie. But Kristie gives him a good income, and she doesn't have to."

"And if she marries Ashton Green?"

"I have no reason to believe that she would cut off Henry. If you knew Kristie, you would know that she just doesn't have that type of malice in her."

"And Ashton?"

She dragged herself up from the settee. "I think you had better go now, Mr Shannon. I have to go out." She walked over to the door, and I followed her back down the hall and out into the garden.

She didn't say goodbye, but at least she hadn't slammed the door. It was either my interviewing technique that was not very good or the Green family were not very nice people. Whatever I had said about Kristie's mum and her relationship with her father had certainly touched a few raw nerves.

CHAPTER TWELVE

I knocked Shoddy's door when I got home, and when he opened it with a can of cheap supermarket beer in his hand, I assumed that he was drunk.

"Been busy today have we?" I attempted unsuccessfully to keep the sarcasm out of my voice.

Shoddy picked up on my mood. As I walked past him, he said bitterly. "This is the first of the day if you must know. I have been running around like a blue-arsed fly trying to get some of the information you needed."

"We needed, "I corrected. "If you haven't forgotten, we are partners. You do the intelligent stuff, and I do the legwork and occasionally get beaten up."

"You sound as if you have had a good day." He handed me a can of beer as if it was a peace offering. I took it and sat down.

"Yeah, sorry, mate. It hasn't been that great a day." I filled him in on the details, and he finished off two cans before I had got to the bit when I arrived at the house of Verna Gibbs.

"It looks like we have come to a dead end, Shod, unless you have something."

"So what you are mainly saying is that you think that Ashton Baxter is a person also known by the name of Harper."

"That's right, so maybe you can try and dig something up on this Harper person and see if what I've been told is correct."

Shoddy didn't look convinced. "I will try, but getting information on international criminals takes time. Croxley police station is hardly linked to New York. I have to rely on a couple of mates telexing people and waiting for a reply. They have to be very careful as well because most of this stuff is monitored and they have to justify why they are asking questions. They can't very well turn around to the desk sergeant and say that they are doing it as a favour for me."

I handed him the folder that Nina Page had given me. "This might help."

He glanced through it quickly and tossed in onto the coffee table. I'll take a closer look later. It's all very complicated dealing with the Yanks.

"Just try your best, mate." I took another can of beer and waited for him to deliver what he'd found out. I knew Shoddy like the back of my hand, and could see from the look on his face that he had found out something relevant, but I had to wait. He leisurely rolled himself a cigarette, popped another can open and settled back in his favourite chair. Finally, he spoke.

"I've been pretty busy myself. I got the information about Ashton Baxter, and after what you just said about him and Harper being the same person, it begins to make sense."

"Go on."

"Well, firstly Ashton Baxter may live in New York, but he is not American. Not fully anyway. It could be that one of his parents was, but he is British as far as his passport is concerned."

"You got to look at his passport?"

"I got to look at his passport application, but not for very long, so I could only scan through it quickly. The good thing is that I found out he has got a juvenile record of thieving and did six months for pimping. He seems to have disappeared off the police radar in the Britain, but has been investigated by the IRS."

"What's that?"

"That is the American equivalent of our Inland Revenue. If those bastards get their hooks in you, they don't let go. Apparently, they suspected that Ashton Baxter was making money by illegal means but couldn't prove anything. Oh, and by the way, he has been married twice, and both of his wives have died in suspicious circumstances."

"Were they rich?"

"How did you guess? Two women older than he was, that had inherited money from their wealthy husbands that had died. But that's not all. Ashton has known links with the American Mafia and was suspected of being a middleman in setting up arms deals between the underworld and terrorist organisations including the IRA, ETA, and the Arab Liberation Front."

"Busy man. How old is he?"

"From his passport application his age is 56."

"So what we are saying is that Ashton is a bad bugger, who will do just about anything to make money. That still doesn't tell me what his interest is with Kristie Green."

"It could be he is trying to clean her out of money. We need to find out what his plan is and try to stop it."

"So what you are saying is that Henry Green is right about Ashton and that he is not just trying to protect his interests."

"There could be a little bit of both going on, but certainly, Kristie looks like she is about to be scammed."

"So what should my next step be?"

"Let's get something to eat, and then maybe you should put the house under surveillance and follow them around for a bit, or even go inside when there is nobody in and take a look around. Either way, I would keep close by her side. If he is going to make a move, then it should be sooner than later."

I had to admit that Shoddy was right. I hate surveillance as it is mind-numbingly boring, but sometimes you just had to do it, when there were no other leads to follow.

I ate some fish cakes and potatoes and headed out to the sleepy village of Barnston. Shoddy cut me some chicken sandwiches and a flask of tea for my vigil, then settled down to read the Charlie Steel file.

CHAPTER THIRTEEN

It was close to 10 o'clock when I got to the Gables and as if they had been waiting for my arrival the little Renault 5 came through the gate of the property before I had a chance to switch off my engine and settle down with my newspaper. There were two people in the car and when they passed me neither of them took the slightest bit of notice. I turned the Elf around and followed at a discreet distance. We travelled for about ten minutes before he pulled into the car park of the Fox and Hounds, just like he had done the last time that I followed him. I wasn't going to make the same mistake that Charlie Steel had done. I waited until Ashton and Kristie had got out of the Renault and entered the pub.

It was at times like these that I wished that I wasn't so tall as it was virtually impossible for me to blend into the background in a room. As they had both seen me before, if the pub was empty, I might as well have gone in bought a drink and sat down at their table. In short, I would have stuck out like a bacon sandwich at a bar mitzvah unless I could come up with a plan.

I walked over to the pub and discreetly looked through the window. It was fairly full, and I couldn't see either of them. I walked around the back and stood in the deserted beer garden scanning the lounge through a small window that had a net curtain with just enough of a crack for me to see Ashton. He was sitting with a half pint of beer in front of him, talking to a man in a pinstripe suit. I couldn't see Kristie as she must have been in the corner. The man in the suit occasionally looked in her direction and said something. There was nothing more for me to do in the beer garden. I couldn't hear what they were discussing, so I made my way back to the Elf and waited for them to come out. When they appeared at closing time, the man in the pinstripe got into flashy BMW and drove off. I followed behind, praying that he didn't open her up and leave me for dead.

As it happened, he was a slower driver than me, and I eventually came to a halt outside a Holiday Inn near Liverpool city centre. Pinstripe man got out, and some flunky drove his car away, but not before I had written down the number.

By the time I got back to my flat, it was after midnight, but I still gave Shoddy a knock on the off chance that he was up. He was watching a late night horror movie, so I quickly told him the number, said that I needed it urgently and left the rest to him. As I climbed exhausted into bed, I hoped that by the time I got up, he would have the man's name, but with Shoddy you could never be sure of anything.

"You're having a laugh. That's the dumbest thing I've ever heard." We were eating breakfast in Shoddy's flat, and he was telling me about what he had found out about Harper.

"That's the name the newspaper chose not me, Moggs."

"So they called him 'The Black Rose Killer?'"

"You know what papers are like; they try to stick some stupid name on everything so that people can get some kind of handle on the story."

"Yes, but Black Rose Killer? What sort of a name is that?"

"It checks out on what your lady friend was saying and the report off Charlie Steel."

"You mean Nina Page? And she's not my lady friend. So what you are telling me is that Harper is this Black Rose Killer."

"I checked up on the death of Rudi Page. He was found poisoned in a hotel bedroom in Clamart, which is just outside Paris. He was lying on the bed with a red rose stuck in his mouth. The autopsy traced the cause to cyanide. Within 24 hours the body of a woman was found hanging from a tree in a forest near the Park Asterix off the A1 near Paris. She also had a rose stuffed into her mouth and had died before Rudy. The local French paper that covered the story gave the killer a name and it was picked up internationally. The story didn't run for very long, though, as there were no arrests and no other incidents."

"So that's it. All you could find out is that Ashton Baxter, alias Harper also has a preference for leaving roses in his victim's mouths."

"Black roses to be exact."

"Yeah, that makes a big difference. Red, white, black, it doesn't give me anything to go on."

Shoddy sighed and poured out the tea. "Well, what about this then. That car you were following last night belongs to a Mr Adam Sweet."

"And?"

"He is the owner of The Irish Club in Breeze Hill."

"That's Walton isn't it?" Shoddy nodded. "Now that's about as rough as they get."

"I've also got an address for Sweet in Aintree, so what the hell was he doing at the Holiday Inn?"

"He could have been meeting somebody, Shod."

"Either way, Moggsy, it looks like Kristie Green has not met the man of her dreams."

"You're right; he's more like the stuff that nightmares are made of. Should I go and tell her?"

"Do you think that she'd believe you?

He was right. Without proof, she would probably think that I was lying. "So what do you think the next step is then?"

"I think you should go and see Adam Sweet and ask him a few questions. If he knows somebody is on to him, then maybe they will back off Kristie."

"The direct approach, eh, Shod?"

"It could work."

"And I could end up getting a good kicking or worse."

"You'll have the element of surprise, and he won't be sure how many other people know, so he will not be inclined to get violent."

"You hope."

"Well, yes, that's the theory behind it, but you can never tell. Besides, I believe you get a terrific pint of draught Guinness down there and authentic Irish Whisky."

"So why not come and try some with me?"

"You know me, Moggs; I'm the thinker behind the operation. You do the legwork. It's worked in the past, and I don't think we should change it."

I finished my tea and looked at my watch. It was just gone midday. I picked up my car keys from off the table. "Ok, I'll give it a go. Breeze Hill you say? If I'm not back by teatime call the cops

"Or Alcoholics Anonymous," quipped Shoddy.

I flicked him the finger as I went through the door, knowing full well that, he would be heading to the pub as soon as I had pulled out of the car park. There were ups and downs to having an alcoholic partner, and I recognised the gleam in his eye when he had mentioned Guinness and the way he had run his tongue across his lips when he told me about the whisky. I only hoped that he would keep the drinking to a minimum, but knowing Shoddy this was not very likely.

CHAPTER FOURTEEN

I drove down theA5058 and picked up Breeze Hill just after the junction with the A5038. There was no sign telling you that the road now had a name, just endless rows of grey council houses and jacked up Ford Cortina's in driveways. This place made Croxley look posh, and I had no illusions of what type of establishment the Irish Club was going to be.

The club was set back off the road in its own car park. It was a large half-timber half brick one storey building that looked in need of a good torching. Some evil looking children were riding around the front door with hoods pulled over their heads on stolen mountain bikes.

I parked the Elf as near to the entrance as I could and made a show of locking the doors, though I couldn't image that anybody in their right minds would consider stealing it or trying to rob the contents. The only thing of value inside the cabin was the radio, and this had never worked since I bought the car. Sometimes there were advantages to driving a wreck.

I worked my way through an invisible crowd milling around the foyer and found an old lady playing a slot machine in the corner. I tried to engage her in conversation about how to get signed in, but she was either death or so engrossed in her game that she completely ignored me. Finally, I took the direct approach and pushed through the door into the bar.

I was immediately confronted by a creature dressed like a doorman. From the out-to-lunch look in his eyes, I could see that he wasn't the brains behind the operation, and I asked if I could talk to the manager. The question seemed to throw him out of his comfort zone, and when I tried to pass him, he put his hand up to my chest and pushed me back against the door.

I wasn't expecting them to welcome me with open arms and kisses, but considering that he didn't know who I was, he seemed to be a little over the top. I was just considering hitting the bastard when I saw Sweet at the far side of the room.

"Mr Sweet, "I called.

He turned, and his gaze came to an abrupt halt on my face. I could instantly feel his dislike. He didn't change his expression and didn't seem to communicate anything to the hired heavy, but he dropped his hand and moved to one side to let me go by. I walked across the room, passed the early afternoon drinkers and came to a halt in front of Sweet. Up close he had a boozers face with heavy jowls and yellow jaundice eyes. He was wearing the same pinstriped suit that he had on the night before though this time I noticed that it had a button missing, and there was a slight tear on the breast pocket.

He spoke with a Northern Irish accent. "What can I do for you, friend?" He didn't offer me his hand. Maybe he thought I was about to sell him double glazing or life assurance. When I told him that I was a private investigator and was looking for information on Ashton Baxter, he looked suitable stunned, which was the desired effect that I wanted. I pressed home my advantage.

""I've been hired by a client to look into his relationship with a Kristie Green, and I thought that maybe you could throw some light on the subject."

"So where do you think that I fit in Mr..."

"Shannon, "I said, handing him a card.

"Why do you think that I should know anything about their relationship?"

"Because you were seen drinking with the two of them in the Fox and Hounds in Barnston last night. Are you denying you were there?"

"I'm not denying anything to you, Mr Shannon. Where I drink and who I talk to is my business, but I would be very careful about where you put that nose of yours. It might get bitten off if you upset the wrong type of people."

"Are you threatening me, Mr Sweet?"

"I am indeed, lad. And by the time you leave this club and head home for your afternoon snooze, I will have all the information that I need on you to make sure that if I see you hanging around me and your man, Ashton Baxter again, you will be severely hurt. Is that clear?"

"So you're not going to offer me a drink then?"

He turned around and walked away, shouting as he was going through a door at the back of the club, "Kenny there is a terrible smell in here, can you show, Mr. Shannon out please."

The Neanderthal walked over and stood a couple of feet away from me. I knew that he would have enjoyed hitting me, but I wasn't in the mood for confrontation. I walked out, and as I was driving out of the car park, I spotted Sweet looking at me from a window in the bar. The meeting hadn't been a success, though it did tell me one or two things. Firstly I had to be careful when dealing with Ashton and his associates, and secondly, I didn't think that Kristie was in a particularly safe position. Sweet was touchy enough to be involved in something not only big but also illegal. I hoped that I hadn't pushed him hard enough for him to do something against me, and wondered if what I had just done would in any way put Kristie in greater danger.

CHAPTER FIFTEEN

As I walked into my office, the first thing that I noticed lying on the floor was an A4 brown envelope. I picked it up and saw that it had been posted in Liverpool the day before. I ripped it open and took out a black and white photo. It showed a younger version of Jenson James, naked with a scantily clad woman straddling him in a huge double bed. His face was clearly recognisable and from his expression, he seemed to be enjoying himself. The woman had her back to the camera, and I could only see the side of her face, but it was enough for me to realise that she was stunningly beautiful. The two of them weren't posing for the photo, which led me to believe that they didn't know it was being taken.

Two questions immediately sprang to mind. Who had sent me the photo and why? I threw it on my desk and checked the answer phone for messages. There was nothing of interest. I needed to talk to Jenson James and see what he would say after I showed him the picture. I hadn't got his address, but a phone call to directory enquiries provided me with all of the information I needed. He lived out in the well-to-do area of Crosby, which was about a half an hour drive away. I decided that I might as well get it over with and hit the road. It was just after three o'clock, as I fired up the Elf and headed for the A565, which would take me to my destination. The address I had written down was a little bit before Crosby, in a district call Thornton.

Jenson's house was detached and set in about an acre of grounds. I pulled the Elf up across the road. The building showed no signs of activity, but there was the yellow E-Type Jaguar parked up at the front. The gate was open, so I walked in, rang the bell and waited. I rang again, and then on an impulse tried the door, which to my complete surprise opened. I walked into the hall and shouted "Hello, anybody at home. Mr James?"

I could hear the sound of a television behind a door at the end of the hall, so I walked towards it. For no apparent reason, I began to feel apprehensive. When I got to the door, I tapped gently and shouted again, "Mr James? Hello; anybody at home?"

I opened the door and popped my head around the gap I had created. Jenson James was lying on the kitchen floor wearing some expensive looking silk pyjamas. He was either fast asleep or dead, but I suspected the latter due to a bullet hole in his throat and the blood all around his head. It was the black rose stuffed into his mouth that made my hair stand on end and the creaking of a floorboard upstairs that made me alert to the fact that it was possible I was not alone in the house. I walked back down the hall and looked up the stairs. These old houses were full of strange noises and the creaking of wooden timbers. I let out a long breath, backed out, opened the front door, and then walked slowly to the car.

When I was safely seated, I sat and watched the house for a good half an hour before finding a call box and phoning the police. I didn't give my name and slammed the receiver down when the operator asked for my details. I had enough experience with the Merseyside police force to know that if I had told them who I was, they would have tried their best to pin the blame on me.

As I headed home, I knew that, as a professional detective, I should have gone into the kitchen examined the body and taken a look around the house. In a situation like that, though, the rules can go out of the window, and what chance would I have had, if the killer was still inside with a pistol? I wasn't being paid enough to put my life on the line, and even if I were, I probably would have done the same.

I drove back to Croxley and stopped off at the office before heading for home. It was a spur of the moment decision that was to alter the course of the next couple of days. I had only sat down at my desk for less than a minute when the phone rang as if somebody had been waiting for me to make myself comfortable. I didn't recognise the voice.

"Is that you, Shannon?"

"Yes," I answered defensively.

"Mr Shannon, it's Nina Page here." It took me a couple of seconds to remember that she was the lady who had hired Charlie Steel to find the person who had killed her husband, Rudi."

"What can I do for you, Mrs Page?"

"It's Charlie. He's come back and wants to meet you. If it is not too inconvenient would it be possible for you to come now?"

"Are you still at the Four Bridges?"

She hesitated. "Er, no we thought that it would be better if we moved to somewhere a bit more secluded. I have rented a holiday cottage in Formby. Do you know the area?"

"Give me the address, and I can be there in about thirty minutes."

I wrote down the address and told her that I was on my way. At least Charlie was alive, and my worst fears for the guy had been put to rest. I wondered what he had been through since the last time we met, and if he knew anything about the murder of Jenson James.

Before leaving, I telephoned Shoddy and told him about my day. He said that the local radio news had been talking about a murder that had taken place in Thornton and that he had been worried that it might have been me. I assured him that I was very much alive, for the moment, and filled him in about the picture. He immediately said that this must be something to do with blackmail, and I was inclined to agree. I shoved the picture into my jacket pocket, grabbed my keys and headed for the door, after telling Shoddy not to wait up.

CHAPTER SIXTEEN

I drove back along the same route I had taken earlier to Thornton, and I passed several police cars on the way before I turned off onto the B439 and headed for the address I had been given in Formby. I stopped off for hamburger and chips at a Wimpy Bar on the way, and when I eventually arrived outside the house it was clouding over and getting dark. It was one of those typical summer evenings on Merseyside that I loved.

Nina Page answered the door. She was wearing a black Kimono, and her long hair was wet as if she had just stepped out of the shower.

"Charlie's out the back on the patio," she said

For somebody who claimed that she had lost all of her money, she certainly seemed to have enough to rent something luxurious. The house was done out completely in brilliant white, and the furniture was modern with a minimalist style that ran through from the hall, lounge and into the kitchen, which was the route I took to get to the patio. It seemed to be the sort of place you would rent for a romantic weekend if you were trying to impress your new girlfriend. What the definition of no money was for Nina Page was probably a lot of money to a normal person.

I tried the kitchen door to get outside and found that it was locked.

"Is that you Nina?" Shouted Charlie.

"Not unless she's grown a set of balls," I called back.

I heard him chuckle as he opened the door to let me out. "You can't be too careful in our business."

I walked through onto the patio, and he shook my hand. He was wearing an old grey sweater with jeans, and his right wrist was bandaged. I also noticed that there was some slight bruising around his left eye.

"You look as if you've been in the wars," I said pulling up a chair and sitting down by the whisky bottle on the table. He joined me and poured us both a generous shot.

"It was touch and go I can tell you. I almost thought I wasn't going to make it."

"I found your car, Charlie, up near Baxter's house. There was blood on the steering wheel, and I assumed the worst."

He found this amusing. "You mean that you thought I was dead? Classic! I am going to put that in my book when I write my life story."

"Talking about stories, Charlie, I would be interested to hear yours for the last couple of days."

He freshened my glass, and I remembered the picture and got it out of my pocket. "Before you start, you might be interested in taking a look at this." I put the envelope on the table and pushed it over.

He put his whisky glass down on it. "Oh, that. It was me that posted the picture to you as a guarantee, in case something had happened to me."

"A guarantee of what?"

"Well, as we both had the same interests in nailing Ashton Baxter, I thought if you were armed with some visual evidence, then you could sort the bastard out if I wasn't in a position to."

"I couldn't make out what was so significant in the picture. It was just a bloke called Jenson James with a woman."

"If you shut up and listen for a minute, Morris, all will be revealed."

I sat back and finished off my drink. At least it was single malt, and the bottle was almost full. "Go on," I said, holding out my glass for a refill. He obliged and sat back himself.

"For a start, Harper or if you want to call him by the name he is using now, Ashton Baxter, is no more of an American than you or I. He has spent a lot of time out there but he has spent a lot of time in many places, usually ripping people off. That day after I left you, I decided to go back to his house and break in. I would have still done it if Ashton had been in, but as luck would have it, both he and the girl left around seven o'clock in the evening, so I had the place to myself. It's where I found the picture. I'm not sure, but it was with a lot of videos so maybe that picture and the others that I found were stills of the videotapes. I took a handful of pictures and just a couple of video tapes with me. I'll give one to you in a minute, and you can take it with you to have a look. It's pretty heavy stuff, but it gives you an idea of what Ashton is up to."

"And just what is that?"

"I can't be certain, but I think the connection with Adam Sweet...."

"Yeah, I had the pleasure of talking to him today, and he was with Baxter and Kristie the other night in the pub..."

"Adam Street is a nasty piece of work and has known IRA connections. I think that the porn videos and the meetings with Sweet point to some sort of IRA funding exercise. I could be wrong, but another thing that I discovered is that something big is going down in Anglesey this weekend, and I need backup if I want to find out what it's all about. Do you want to be that backup, Morris?"

I wasn't sure where all this was leading, but it was certainly taking on a bigger vibe than just digging up a little bit of dirt on Kristie Green's boyfriend. I stalled for time; "So how come there was blood on the steering wheel of your car, Charlie?"

"I was coming out of the house and decided rather than make my way through the woods, to take the quicker way and go over the wall. I forgot that it had broken glass on the top, and I cut my wrist, fell off and gave myself a real shiner of an eye. I got back to my car safely enough, but who should go past as I was just about to go home, but Ashton with his girlfriend. It was a delayed reaction. He must have remembered the car about thirty seconds after he had driven past. I saw his brake lights go on, and he started to do a three point turn. We were in a deserted part of the countryside; I was driving a Fiesta, and he was driving a Cosworth Supercar. I knew that I could never outrun him and that he was probably packing a pistol. What could I do? I got out of the car and ran into the woods. I don't think that he attempted to follow me, but I didn't hang around to check. I kept on the move slept rough for the night and then got in contact with Nina. She said she would move out of the hotel and rent somewhere more secluded, and that she would come and pick me up. And that, as they say, is the story. What do you think of it so far?"

"Not a lot," I replied mechanically. He filled up my glass and waited for my questions.

"So are you saying that Ashton was blackmailing Jenson James?"

"I don't think so because James has never been married. A solicitor in bed with a woman? Where is the scandal in that? If you look at the picture, it looks like James is very young. He was probably a student. The woman is much older. Maybe he had just been paid to make a sex film, and Ashton was marketing it. I tell you, Morris, there was a shelf full of sex videos. I stopped counting at fifty, and there were two more shelves."

"So what you are saying is that we still don't know that much."

"What I'm saying is that the only thing I have that is definite is an entry in Baxter's desk diary for this Saturday. There is an old disused airfield near Holyhead in Anglesey, and I intend to be there. Are you with me, Morris?"

I grudgingly nodded my head. I certainly didn't want to get tied up in a conflict with the Irish Republican Army. I was almost killed by one of their operatives early on in my career and had never forgotten the feeling you get when you are certain that any minute somebody is going to put a bullet in your head.

He disappeared into the house and came back out with a video tape marked XXX. He handed it to me. "Here, take a look at this and see if you can get any information. It's pretty blue I'm afraid, but just imagine what it must be like working in the vice squad. They must have to watch hundreds of these things. I also took these snapshots of Ashton. I have an appointment tomorrow in Paris, which may throw some light on him being the person who murdered Nina's husband." He handed me a couple of grainy pictures showing in one Ashton getting into his car, and in the other one, Ashton, and Kristie Leaving the house.

"An appointment in Paris?"

"Yes, I'm flying out from Liverpool and coming back the same day."

"You must have something pretty important lined up to go all that way."

"I can tell you that when I come back, but I've got my fingers crossed."

I drained my glass and made my way to the door. Nina must have gone to bed because she wasn't around as I was leaving. I told Charlie that I would get back in touch before the weekend, and he thanked me for offering to help. I couldn't remember giving him a firm offer of anything, but as I walked back to the Elf, I realised that this case had taken on a whole new dimension, and was fast getting further and further out of my league.

I was home by eleven-thirty and asleep by midnight.

CHAPTER SEVENTEEN

The next morning in Shoddy's flat, I gave him the video and told him that he needed to watch it and look for any clues that might help with my enquiry. His eyes nearly popped out of his head when he saw the XXX on the cassette and said that he would clear the morning to do it. When I left, I don't think I had ever seen him happier to do some research.

I picked up a local newspaper and read it while I ate bacon and eggs for breakfast at a local greasy spoon cafe. The front page was full of the murder of local solicitor Jenson James. The story continued onto the centre pages and went into his personal life and all of the work that he did for charities in Croxley. There was no mention of the black rose stuffed into his mouth, and no talk of suspects, except to say that it may have been a disgruntled client.

I had an appointment with Henry Green at 12 o'clock and I headed to the address he had given me on the outskirts of Knowsley. A lady who looked like a housekeeper answered the door and showed me into a very grand study. She told me the Mr Green would be with me in a minute. I stood by the window admiring the stripe lines that had been mown into the plush lawn. Green was either a keen gardener or he was paying somebody a lot of money to keep the grass in this condition.

Green arrived about five minutes into my stay, and just when I was getting bored with his flower beds. He indicated that I should sit down on the plain wooden chair in front of his desk, while he took a plush revolving armchair behind it. My chair was subtly lower than his and slightly too small to go with the office furniture. I wondered if he had done this deliberately to make visitors feel uneasy.

"So what have you got for me, Mr Shannon?"

He didn't waste time with niceties when it came to the hired help.

"I have got one or two findings to report and a couple of questions that maybe you could answer."

"Ok, let me have you report first."

"Firstly, I do think that Kristie is in danger and that Ashton Baxter is involved in some criminal activities."

He nodded his head and looked pleased but didn't say anything.

"I did speak to Kristie, and she told me to mind my own business. She also called you are a nasty man for prying into her affairs. I also made contact with Baxter and found out a few things about him. Did you know that he wasn't American?"

"No, I didn't."

"One thing also that you forgot to inform me about, Mr Green, is that you are not Kristie's natural father."

That wiped the smile off his face. "I didn't think that was relevant. In every other way, I have been a father to her, and she calls me dad. Don't you think that this is enough?"

In fact, I didn't, but I let it go for the moment, and pushed the brown envelope containing the picture, across the desk. "Does this ring any bells with you, Mr Green?"

He took the picture out of the envelope, and his face became distorted with rage. He got up out of his seat and threw it back at me. "How dare you, show me something like this. What sort of a scumbag are you?"

I got up myself, and immediately the atmosphere between us changed, as now I towered over him by a good six inches. "I'm the scumbag that you hired to help you get information on Ashton. That picture is part of the process. Now, are you going to tell me if you can enlighten me about what it is, or are you just going to say that you haven't got a clue what it's all about."

He sat back down, deflated. When he spoke, it was almost as if he was talking to himself. "The man is my lawyer, Jensen James, and the woman is my wife."

I sat down and gave him some time to get himself back under control. The picture had shocked him, as it would any normal person. "I'm sorry, Mr Green, for having to dig up the past, but did you know that Jenson James was having an affair with you, wife?"

"Look at the age of Jenson, man; he was at university when this picture was taken. It was years before I met either of them."

"So just how did you meet your wife, Mr Green?"

He seemed to shake himself out of self-pity and got up from his chair again. "You have a mind like an open sewer, Shannon."

"I'm just doing my job, Mr Green."

"I want to thank you for the work you have done for me, but to be frank, I don't think that you are any good at your job, and I will go to a bigger and more professional agency to carry on with my investigations into Ashton Baxter. I trust that I don't owe you any more money?"

"No, you're up to date on that."

"Then I'll bid you good day." With that, he walked out.

CHAPTER EIGHTEEN

When I got back to Shoddy's flat, he was in an excited state, in more ways than one. He told me that he had watched the video four times and that there was something that he wanted me to have a look at. He also told me that Charlie Steel had phoned and told him that I was to meet him at five o'clock that coming Saturday. Shoddy had written down the address. Charlie had told him that after watching another one of the videos, he had come up with some information that would, in his expression, 'blow my mind.' He didn't say what, though, but he did tell me to call his boss Nina Page about payment for my help.

She answered the phone on the second ring. "Mr Shannon, is that you?"

"You are very sure of yourself Mrs Page; it could have been anybody calling."

"There are only two people that have this number, Mr Shannon and Charlie is the other one. As I have just spoken to him, I used my powers of deduction."

"You should be a detective." The silence on the other side of the line showed that she wasn't into swapping flippant comments. I made a mental note to keep it strictly about business when I talked to her in future. I started again and put some respect in my voice as I hoped she was going to be my next employer. "You wanted to speak to me?"

"Mr Shannon, I was speaking to Charlie, and he indicated that the job was getting too big for him to carry out on his own. I am not a rich person, but I want to get some closure on the man who killed my Rudi. Are you willing to work for me?"

I wondered what sort of closure she was thinking about for Ashton. Nothing less than the closure of life itself looked as if it was going to satisfy this woman. I didn't want to get involved in any assassination plot no matter how bad the man had been. She told me how much she was prepared to pay me to work with Charlie at the weekend, and I mentally whistled and accepted. It was after I put the phone down that I realise the magnitude of what I had lined up for myself on the island of Anglesey. If it was the IRA, then I was dealing with killers. Maybe I should have told her I needed to think it over and consulted with Shoddy. I looked at my partner, slowing down and going backwards and forwards with the video. There was a woman with her mouth open in ecstasy and a young stud pumping away in slow motion from behind.

"Take a closer look at this Moggsy," called Shoddy

"It looks interesting enough from here, thank you."

"Not the anal sex bit, I'm looking at the bedside table and the key on the side."

He stopped the video in a place where both occupants of the bed had very comical expressions on their faces. He went into one of his cupboards, brought out a magnifying glass and went back over to the TV. "I can't quite make it out, Moggs; can you come over and take a look, you've got younger eyes than me." He handed me the magnifying glass and pointed to a key on a key ring shaped like a penis that was on the bedside table. Can you read what it says?"

I tried to get the best position to see the writing, but it was difficult. "It looks like fat tidy?"

"Or is it fat titties," quipped Shoddy.

"Fantasy," we both shouted at the same time.

"The Fantasy Massage Parlour in Litherland."

"Shit! Is that place still going after all these years," I said

"I was busting the tarts in that place when I was in uniform walking the beat, still wet behind the ears," replied Shoddy "The Fantasy Club, I remember it well; a massage a shag and a dose of the pox."

Shoddy was howling with laughter now. "Yep, even by some of the depths massage parlours plunged to in the early seventies on Merseyside that place was number one for getting ripped off and a serious medical condition. You know what the keys were for don't you?"

I shook my head.

"They were so used to getting raided that the girls would lock themselves with their clients in the rooms, and if the police arrived they would both jump out through the window. The thing is, those penis shaped key rings were dead giveaways, but the owner of the place said that only a dirty mind would see them as a man's cock and that they were artistic monoliths. What was her name now?" Glenda? Gwen...?"

"Glenys," I said

"That's the one; Glenys. She acted all posh and high-class, but underneath she was as dirty as they come; like a bitch on heat. The lads used to say that she would perform any perversion for a tenner. They called her 'red hat and no knickers' down the station, because of her Sloan Square accent. I wonder what she's doing now."

"She was no spring chicken twenty years ago. She's probably dead."

"Or retired to the Caribbean; that place was bad, but they certainly had a lot of customers.

"Mainly Russian sailors if I remember correctly. Those lads would shag anything."

"Do you think it's worth a trip to see what I can find out?"

"I wouldn't do any harm, but you're not coming back in here, if it is still open, without having a shower first." It was my turn to laugh. I looked at my watch; it was a little after three pm. "I tell you what, make something to eat and I will go and see if it is open tonight. If I remember, correctly they never did anything during the day.

"So what do you want to eat? I've got pilchards and fish fingers in the fridge, or do you want to go to the fish and chip shop and get us a takeaway."

I didn't take that much thinking about. "I'm on my way. Warm the plates in the oven, and make the tea. I'll be back in about ten minutes."

CHAPTER NINETEEN

Before I left for the Fantasy, Shoddy handed me another A4 picture. It was one taken by the police photographer of Jenson James with a black rose stuck in his mouth. I slipped it into the envelope with the other photograph and set off for Litherland. I remembered roughly where the club used to be, but I wasn't expecting it to have possibly survived. I parked the Elf on Phoenix Road and got out and walked. The boarded up houses and shops that I passed made me even more pessimistic that I had come on a wasted journey, but to my surprise there it was. Number 17, still bore the name of The Fantasy Massage Parlour, and it hadn't changed a bit. It was still as decrepit looking as it was when I was a teenager.

I rang the bell, and the small mouse like woman who opened it looked like her sixtieth birthday was a distant memory. She was heavily made up, but still good looking in a perverse sort of way. She had two gold teeth at the front of her mouth and huge dark rings around her eyes that made her look like a panda. She was dressed entirely in black and had a heavy perfume smell that hung around her that reminded me of sex juices gone stale.

I tried my luck

"Glenys?"

She fumbled in the pocket of her cardigan, brought out a pair of glasses, put them on and examined me. Finally, she said. "That's me, Luv, though I don't do massages anymore, and by the look of you, son, you need somebody a bit more energetic. Call back later when we're open and I'll get you fixed up with somebody nice." She tried to shut the door, but I put my foot in it.

"My name is Morris Shannon. I'm a private investigator, and I was wondering if I could ask you a few questions." I got out my ID and offered it to her. She ignored it.

"If you're police, you get it for half price, now get your fucking foot out of my door, and come back later."

I leaned in, lifted her up and carried her into the hall, closing the door after me with my foot. She was surprisingly light even for her size, and she didn't resist or scream but seemed to enjoy the ride. I went into my pocket and brought out the envelope with the pictures inside. I held it up for her to see. "This will only take a couple of minutes. I have some pictures in here, and just want you to take a look."

She straightened her clothing and ran her fingers through her hair, making a show that she hadn't been phased by what I had just done. "I'd better take a look then, Luv."

I held both pictures up. She pointed to the one in the bedroom. "That was taken here, a good few years ago, though."

"Do you know who the people are?"

"Don't know who the woman is, but she's got a nice arse. I would certainly hire her. The man is Jenson James. He's the stiff in the other picture as well. The black rose in the mouth goes well. It couldn't have happened to a nicer bloke."

"Can you shed any light on the picture?"

"I don't know what you mean, Luv. You do talk posh don't you?"

"You said that you didn't know the woman. So what is she doing in one of your bedrooms?"

"From time to time during the 1970s I used to get asked by some lads from Liverpool, to hire out a room for them to do porn videos. They paid well, so what could a working girl do but accept."

"Can you remember the name of the man who paid you?"

She shook her head. "I can't even remember what I watched on TV last night, never mind ten years ago. I know Jenson because he used to play the part of the stud sometimes and would often call in for a massage as well. I don't remember her, though." She put her glasses on again and examined the photo closely." "Now I could make a fortune off an arse like that. What are the tits like, Luv, have you seen them?"

"I'm sorry, Glenys, I can't say that I have."

"Then that's all I that I can say I'm afraid. Did you say that you wanted a massage?" She moved her fingers suggestively. "You a big bloke aren't you. Maybe I could come out of retirement for the night."

"I'm sorry, but I've got a load of appointments tonight. Maybe some other time."

"Half price."

She was persistent, and I began to make my way through the door. This lady scared the shit out of me. She was older than my mother. I got out onto the pavement again and regained some of my confidence.

"So is there a name that you can give me of anyone involved in those movies."

"Apart from Jenson?"

"Yeah, obviously apart from him because he's dead."

She thought about it for a moment. "There was Alisha."

"What about Alisha?"

"Most of the time, these people would arrive with a film crew and actors, but there was one time when they were short of a girl. I don't know, but somebody hadn't turned up or something. I lent them a girl called Alisha, and she filled in for the day. In fact, she left me soon after and went to work for them, though never here. I didn't blame her, the money was a lot better than I was going to pay her, and technically she was in the movies. She may be able to throw more light on the people that she worked for."

"Where can I get hold of her?"

She looked me up and down again like she was examining a piece of meat. "You did say that you would be coming back tomorrow for a massage, didn't you?"

"Yeah, sure; I could do with a good body rub."

"Oh, I'd give you a bloody body rub all right, Luv. One you wouldn't forget in a hurry. Wait here for a minute."

She slammed the door shut in my face, and I waited for at least ten minutes before she reappeared. "Here is Alisha's address. I used to visit her regularly, but I haven't seen her for a couple of years. If you contact her, tell her that Glenys was asking about her."

I thanked her and walked back to my car. The address was Litherland, so I decided to give it a try. Glenys certainly was a character, but wild horses would not have dragged me back to

Phoenix Road for an all over body rub, or anything else that meant

taking my clothes off in the same building that she was in.

CHAPTER TWENTY

They say that Litherland was mentioned in the Doomsday Book in 1086 if I remember correctly from my history classes. That was before even Liverpool existed. The district is part of the Borough of Sefton and not too far from Croxley. When I was in my teens, in the summer holidays, Litherland was the place to come if you wanted to go underage drinking and buy drugs. It was and still is a fairly tough neighbourhood to live in, but I've always liked the banter in the pubs and clubs, even though you get the feeling that you are only a wrong sentence or phrase from getting your head kicked in.

Litherland had never amounted to very much at its most affluent and now most of the shops and houses that were inhabited looked as if they shouldn't be. The damp looking council house in Preston Brook Avenue reflected all that is bad about the area. Angry looking kids riding their bikes around the car parks of the local pub selling weed to customers, and motor cars jacked up on bricks in gardens flooded with engine oil and grease that looked like slag heaps. If this district had been a dog or a cat, it would have been put to sleep years ago.

I sensed the disused atmosphere of the house as I walked up the path. The curtains were drawn and not hung correctly, and the only sign of life was an Alsatian dog chained to the fence. He was eating a huge white bone and didn't seem to notice me. The bone was probably all that was left of the postman. I gave the animal a wide berth and rang the bell, which surprisingly worked.

The door was opened as far as the security chain would allow, by a fat middle-aged woman dressed in an electric green shell suit.

"My name is Morris Shannon. I wonder if I could speak to Alisha Lee."

She seemed puzzled by my question but took the chain off and opened the door. I walked past her into the hallway, which had a kitchen straight ahead and a door on the right, which led into another room. The fat lady went into this room, and I followed. There was a terrible smell of urine and a wheelchair in front of a gas fire that was full on.

"This is Alisha, though I don't think that you are going to get much out of her today. Are you from social services?"

The lady in the chair didn't look at me but was staring into space with her mouth open. Saliva dripped from one corner of her mouth. She had a thin face that looked as if it could have at one time been beautiful, but now it held hardly any expression at all, and only her darting eyes showed any sign that there was a mind at work behind them. "What's wrong with her?"

"So you're not from the social."

"No."

"Then who are you?"

I handed her one of my cards and waited while she read it. She wasn't that quick-brained either and I watched as she mouthed the words of my name and address one by one.

"What does a private detective want with Ali?"

"Well, I did want to ask her a few questions but.....What did you say was wrong with her?"

"She had a stroke last year and has been like this ever since. She can talk a bit when she wants to, but it takes it out of her. My name's

Jo, by the way; I'm a local helper. I come in to do some cleaning get her dressed and cook her meals. I have written to the social services about them giving me some help; I thought you were too good to be true."

"I'm sorry to disappoint you, Jo; I'm sure they will send somebody around eventually. Could I try and talk to her?"

"Help yourself." She folded her arms aggressively and watched me closely as a knelt down by Alisha's chair. I felt like an idiot and a fraud doing this, and I hoped it wasn't going to do her any harm. I held the two pictures up in front of her. "Alisha; do you recognise anybody in these photos?"

Nothing! She wasn't even looking at them. I felt the fat woman's eyes burning into my back and smelt that she had lit up a cigarette. I looked at the spot on the wall that Alisha was staring at. I held the two pictures in front of her again only this time in her eye-line and repeated the question. She didn't say anything, but at least her eyes were now focused where I wanted them to be. Her arms started shaking quite violently. "Is this normal, Jo?"

"She's trying to tell you something."

"What?"

"How do I know? You are going to have to wait to see if she will talk."

I took the pictures away, and she got even more agitated, so I got them back out again and waited. My arms were starting to ache.

"Shall I make a cup of tea," said Jo

"I wasn't planning to stay that long. How much time will this take?"

"You've started it, so I think that the least you can do is wait till she spits out what she wants to say to you. It must be pretty important to her if she has got this worked up. Milk and sugar?"

"Two spoons please and a little milk."

I was on my second cup when Alisha eventually began to talk. It was slow at first and just a garbled mess of sounds. Then, she just shouted out, "Rose." I looked at Jo.

"She does like flowers. Are there any in the pictures?" Before I had a chance to answer, Alisha shouted out Rose, Black," and relaxed back into the chair. By the time I had got up and put the pictures back in the envelope she had gone to sleep.

"That's the exhaustion, dear, of saying those two words. Was there a black rose in the pictures?"

"Yes."

"And was it useful what she said?"

"Er, I'm not sure, but I think that I have overstayed my welcome," I shouted "goodnight, Alisha," as I made my way out, but she was already snoring.

CHAPTER TWENTY-ONE

I popped into the office on my way back home, to check my answer phone and see if I had received any post. Sometimes I don't know why I bother working because all I seem to get is bills, and most of them are final demands. I switched on my answer phone as I was looking at my electricity bill final demand and working out how I was going to pay it.

The tape started to roll. "Hello, Morris, it's Charlie. I'm in a call box with no more change so got to be quick. There have been some mind-blowing developments after my trip. Too many to speak about on your answer phone: get your arse down to Anglesey tonight; it looks like the date has been moved forward. If I am not in the cottage, I will leave you a note telling you where I'll be... Oh and bring some binoculars." The line went dead.

I dialled Shoddy's number every five minutes for half an hour before he eventually picked up. "Hello?" At least he sounded sober.

"Shoddy, it's me. Where the hell have you been?"

"I just nipped out to get us some food in for tonight. Where are you?"

"I'm still at the office, and I need to go to Anglesey this minute. Charlie said that Ashton's on the move."

"Are you sure that the Elf will make it all the way out there?"

"It's going to have to. I'll give you a call and let you know what's happening when I know myself."

"OK, I'm just starting to watch the porn video again to see if I've missed something. I'm sure that there is more to the film that meets the eye. "

"Sounds like a nice evening you've got lined up, partner. Do you want to swap?"

"No, you're OK, but just take care; if it is the IRA, then they will have guns, so if it does get heavy, keep your head down. How did it go at the Fantasy Club?"

I told him briefly about the events of the evening, and about Alisha's obsession with roses. I promised him that I would be very careful, and told him that there was nothing to worry about. I don't think either of us believed that, but I had already taken on the job, so there was no going back, especially after the electric bill I had just received.

It took me an age to find my binoculars, but I was eventually ready and locked up. As I was going down the stairs, I heard the phone ringing. It was a toss-up between going back up the stairs, down the corridor and unlocking my door, or ignoring it and leaving it to the answer phone to pick-up. I chose to ignore it, which in hindsight was the worst thing I could have done. I slammed the outside door and headed for the car.

"Hello, Hello, Moggsy........It's me, Shoddy. For fuck sake pick up, will you? I just saw the end of that video and there is something on there that changes everything, especially after what you just told me ....Where are you? If you hear this message, do not, I repeat, do not go to that house in Anglesey.........."

CHAPTER TWENTY-TWO

When I got to Anglesey, it was closing in on 11 o'clock about as fast as it could. This holiday island off the coast of North Wales is connected by a suspension bridge to the civilised world, and when you cross over it, for some reason I could never explain, you feel like you are stepping back in time to the early 1950s. In Anglesey, there are teddy boys and hippies and the jukeboxes in the pubs still gave you a choice between Bill Hayley and sweet Gene Vincent. On this island, where the beehive and drainpipe trousers are still considered risqué you are never far from the sea or a slice of nostalgia. I headed up the A5, which followed the old Roman road until I passed Llanfairpwllgwyngyll, which is one of the places with unpronounceable names that I'm sure was created by the Welsh to piss off the English.

Out at sea beyond the harbour, a mass of black clouds was moving in from the mainland, and I could feel a strong wind buffering my little Elf making progress rather slow. This part of the A5 was totally straight, but there was very little cover, and I prepared myself for a pretty grim journey towards Holyhead, which is on the far side of the island. The great thing about Anglesey, however, is that in the space of a day you can get all of the seasons of the year rolled into a couple of hours. By the time I passed through the interesting sounding village of Bryngwran, the black clouds had all but disappeared, and a full moon was peeping nervously through broken white fluffy pieces of cotton wool, dangling from an opaque and unfathomable sky. I still wasn't convinced that this was how it was going to stay. With my luck, it would probably be snowing by the time I reached my destination.

With ten miles to go before Holyhead my head was banging with a tension headache and my legs hurt from being wedged into the cabin space of my tiny car like an overgrown sardine. A fighter jet taking off from RAF Valley very nearly sent me hurtling into a tree as its wheels almost touched down on my roof. I'd forgotten about the military base on the island, but that was my wake-up call. I shook the cobwebs out of my brain and looked for the turn off for Penrhos, which according to the address I had been given, was where the cottage was situated. I almost missed the turning, but I reversed and pointed the nose of the Elf down a very dubious looking track towards my destination. Charlie had told Shoddy that it was on the B236 just before you entered the village and it was a semi-detached whitewashed cottage.

I found it so easily I felt cheated. There was no garden, and the front door opened up directly onto the road. As soon as I pulled up in front, I noticed that the door was slightly ajar. I got out of the car and pushed it open all the way and flicked on the light switch. There were marks around the lock that showed it had been jimmied. The first thought that entered my head as always in these situations was that whoever had done this job might still be wandering about inside. I turned off the lights and stood in the hall listening for any sounds. I could hear that the next door neighbours had their TV on quite loud, and it brought a sort of normality to the occasion, but not enough to make me fully relax. My headache had gone, but it had been replaced by nausea brought on by anxiety.

My eyes had got used to the darkness, so I pushed open a door and found myself standing in a neat little country style lounge. There was a standard lamp throwing out a poor substitute for light in the corner. It gave the room and eerie atmosphere, as did Charlie, who was lying on the floor with a pool of blood around his head. I had to look away for a couple of seconds because he had been shot through his left eye and it was not a pretty sight. The obligatory black rose had been stuffed into his mouth giving him a surreal, symbolic vibe that seemed to have been created to bring out fear and the instinct to run away in the mind of the beholder. It was certainly hitting the spot for me, and I had to force myself to take a further look.

Now, as I knelt over the body, I felt another emotion rising inside me; a feeling of waste and total uselessness. Here was a man that I liked, who had been wiped off the spectrum of life on the whim of some evil bastard and there was nothing I could do, besides getting revenge. I closed his eyes, erased sentiment from my thought process and looked around the room. Whoever had done this, must have used a silencer otherwise the house would have been swarming with police by now; unless of course, the neighbours were deaf, or in fact, dead themselves.

On the table, there was a map of the island with a spot that had been marked in red pen as 'Standing Stones Airfield.' On top of the map, again, written in red pen was a short note. It read:

Morris,

I couldn't wait and have gone to the airfield. I will be in position at the top of the steps from the car park. Be as quick as you can. Charlie.

A note Charlie had written before he was about to leave or a trap? This seemed too easy, but all I could do was go with the flow. No other choices sprang to mind. I stuffed the map into my pocket, retraced my steps back to the car and drove off in the direction of Holyhead and my final destination for the evening, which I now knew had something to do with planes.

CHAPTER TWENTY-THREE

I carried on driving towards Holyhead for about three miles and then took a turning signposted Standing Stones. The road was not very well maintained, and the pot holes combined with a mist that was rolling in off the sea made the driving conditions particularly interesting. The road came abruptly to a halt in a parking lot that was nothing more than a sand pit with rickety steps leading up to an embankment. There was just one car in the lot, a black Ford Cosworth. There were plenty of hiding places for my car, in the fields on either side of the road I had just taken, but I didn't have time for all that so I just stopped and got out.

I walked up the steep hill, which ended at the top with a metal-sided shed, big enough to take a small plane. There were several more of the inverted V-shaped constructions dotted about with a pathway that ended in what vaguely looked like a disused runway. I could tell that it was a runway because two were walking up it placing lights on the tarmac. The mist was getting stronger, if a pilot was going to land in this god-forsaken hole, then it must be for something worth a lot of money. I scanned the area with my binoculars. At the side of the runway furthest from where I was standing, there was a wooden shed with a light shining out of an open door. A few metres behind the shed and stretching out into infinity was a chain link and barbed wire perimeter fence that gave the place a prisoner of war camp feel. In the distance, I could just about make out the angry white horses of the waves as they crashed down on the almost pure white sand. The sound drowned out everything else. The runway lights were now in place and shone brightly into space. I scanned the sky for any sign of a plane, but could see nothing. I imagined that during the next half hour the shed was going to be surrounded by a shroud of grey mist, and the beach would disappear. I wondered if this was considered good or bad weather if you were smuggling something in or out of the country.

I settled down on the turf and waited. I occasionally ran my binoculars over the scene below. Every time I looked it got more and more blurred. I wished that I had brought a flask of tea and some sandwiches and hoped that this wasn't going to be a long night. Half an hour later my legs had gone to sleep, and then everything happened at once.

I heard the sound at first, high up in the night sky. The engine sounded like my Riley Elf; I hoped for the pilot's sake that it was better maintained. I saw a single light next, dropping out of the sky far too fast as if it was in a hurry to land. As well as the two men standing by the runway waiting, another figure appeared from out of the shed. All eyes were on the approaching plane, but not mine. I had spotted that the third person was keeping well back, and as the plane circled low over the landing strip, the figure started running towards where I was lying.

With the mist and the noise of the plane's engine mingles with the crashing of the waves, I don't think that anybody noticed except me. The plane reached the concrete apron beside the shed, just as the figure reached me. I jumped up, recognised that it was Kristie Green and pulled her down.

"You've got to help me get away; those men down there are going to kill me." She made an attempt to get up, but I held her down. "Let me go you bastard, didn't you hear what I just said, they will kill you as well if they catch us."

There was a shout from down below. I trained my binoculars on the hut, and could see one of the men running at speed towards us. She was getting hysterical now. "Look, stay here if you want, but I've got to go."

"Ok, I've got my car. Let's go."

She didn't need telling twice but took off and disappeared down the steps leading to the car park. I found it difficult to keep up. When we got to the bottom, she saw the Elf. "Is that your car?" I glanced at the Cosworth and said defiantly.

"It's that or nothing I'm afraid."

She got in the passenger seat, and I got in the other side praying she was going to start. She did on the third attempt, and as we were driving away, I could see the man arriving in the car park from my rear view mirror and floored the accelerator. The Elf responded and the speedometer grudgingly crept up to fifty-five, which was very good considering the age of the engine. I glanced at Kristie; she had tears streaming down her face and was shaking with what I assumed was a release of tension mixed with sheer terror.

"I'm sorry that you're cold, but the heater doesn't work."

She made an attempt to smile. "That's OK; just let's get as far away as possible from those men."

We drove for a while in silence and then the thing that I had been dreading happened. I hated to tell her, but in my mirror, I could see a pair of powerful headlights coming up fast behind us, and on a road as straight as the one we were on, there was no escaping the inevitable. If I didn't do something fast, we were going to be in serious trouble.

CHAPTER TWENTY-FOUR

The mist wasn't thick enough to hide in, and it looked like it was starting to clear. I frantically scanned the rolling hedges on either side of the road for an opening into a field, but there weren't any. Kristie had become very quiet. The sobbing had stopped, but she looked frightened enough to jump out of the car. I slowed down and switched off the lights.

"I'll carry on Kristie, and you get out and hide. I'll try my best to lead them away."

"Look!" she pointed to a gap in the hedge in a parking area just a few feet away on the other side of the road. I drove the Elf towards it. There was a wooden gate that was shut. I slammed on the brakes got out and rushed towards it. The gate was locked, and now the headlights of the approaching car picked up my silhouette against the side of the road. If this was the IRA we were dealing with, then we were dead meat.

The car approached us very fast and carried on past; it was a big white Ford pickup truck and I just about caught sight of a woman driving. Obviously, she was in a rush to get home and knew the road well. I felt the tension drain from my body and got back in the car.

"False alarm."

She smiled weakly at me. "I need to get away from here. These men are animals. I know they are going to kill me." The bottom lip started to tremble, and tears rolled down her face again. I was hopeless when it came to emotional women, especially beautiful ones because they made me feel inadequate. I could never think of the right thing to say, so I didn't bother. It was probably best for her to get the tears out of her system sooner rather than later, but what did I know? I needed to concentrate on getting us out of the mess we were in, and comforting an emotional female would just get in the way.

I eventually did see a gap into a field with an open gate. I drove the Elf inside and stopped at the side of the hedge and turned off the engine. I got out and checked that we were hidden from the road, and satisfied that we were, I got back in.

I turned to Kristie. "Now, could you tell me what this is all about?"

She put her head down and examined her hands. I was in no hurry and leaned back into the driver's seat and waited.

"They are going to kill me."

"Yeah, you told me that bit, Luv. It's all the little bits leading up to your imminent death that interests me at the moment. "Was I being too harsh? To be honest, I was tired, stiff with cramp, in need of food and drink and didn't give a damn.

"I met Ashton by chance in New York, when I was on holiday with my aunt. He was staying in the same hotel, and I recognised him as being somebody that my mother had around the house occasionally. He's only half American; his dad is Irish, from Kilkenny. We hit it off instantly, and sort of had an affair."

I could have queried that Ashton was old enough to be her father, but let it go, and waited for her to continue.

"He's quite mad you know. Scary too. Have you ever been fascinated by someone, Mr Shannon and then realised that they weren't what they seemed?"

"No."

"I moved in with him when we came back to England, and then I met his friends and found out what he was doing."

"And what was that?"

"He was producing sex videos and selling them. The money he was making he gave away to the IRA. His friend Adam Sweet got his money from ripping people off and robbing post offices." She started to cry again but kept on talking. "I didn't know what to do. He told me that he would kill me if I didn't do what he said and that my mother had made him a lot of money doing.....Well, I suppose you know what she did. Dad must have told you that."

"So what was this all about at the airfield?"

"Those men in the plane were coming for me." She leaned over and buried her face in my chest sobbing hysterically. I waited for her to calm down.

"What do you mean coming for you?"

"He'd sold me, Mr Shannon. The bastard had sold me to the Arabs to fund his precious IRA, and the sad thing about it all is that I loved the bastard......I loved him......."

I let her cry it out until there was nothing left. I felt like crying myself. What sort of people were there in this world to do this sort of thing.

She eventually sat up and wiped her eyes with her hand. She reminded me of a small child, and I wanted to father her, and then kill Ashton and Sweet, with my bare hands.

"So what do you want to do, Kristie?"

She seemed calmer now. "I want to get away as far as possible. Take me to the ferry port in Holyhead."

CHAPTER TWENTY-FIVE

It was nearly 4:00 in the morning when I eventually drove over the Anglesey suspension bridge, turned left and picked up the A55 for Colwyn Bay. It was the long road leading home. I had taken Kristie to the ferry port in Holyhead, and she had walked straight on board one of the ships leaving for Dublin. It was almost 3:00 as I sat on the pier and watched her sail into the distance. We had been lucky to catch the 2:30 service and only had done so because it had been delayed by fog. Still, after what Kristie had told me, she was due a bit of luck.

My mind settled back, and I drove on auto pilot as I tried to decide what I was going to tell Henry Green. He had been right about Ashton, but it wasn't the final result that he had hoped for. Or was it? Ashton was now well and truly out of the mix when it came to having a loving relationship with Kristie, so she was free to carry on with her life. I had no doubt that part of that life would include giving Green his allowance. She just didn't seem the sort of a girl who would walk out on her responsibility, though what did I know? I had never been a great judge of character. I passed through Old

Colwyn and was debating whether to stop for something to eat at an all night Little Chef further down the coast when I noticed headlights approaching behind me. There had been virtually no traffic on the A55 for the last half an hour, and I wasn't too concerned at first. It was when the lights arrived about an inch from my back bumper on full beam that I began to suspect that this was not just someone in a hurry to get home.

I was doing around 50 miles an hour and knew that I couldn't squeeze any more speed out of the Elf if I didn't want her to overheat. The car behind overtook and came up alongside. It was the black Cosworth and Ashton was at the wheel. He didn't look very happy and pointed for me to pull over. I slammed on my brakes, and he went shooting passed. The Elf stalled after a few shudders and misfires. I saw the brake lights go on at the back of the Cosworth, and it started to reverse quickly. I couldn't start my car and braced myself for the impending shunt. Ashton expertly stopped just before he hit me and at the same time my engine sprang into life. I spun the wheel and tried to get past him, but he pulled away and kept up with me with ease. He was probably still in second gear. I was not on the wrong side of the road with no chance of outrunning the bastard and every chance of getting hit by a passing juggernaut heading for the ferry port.

I saw the lights of the all night cafe coming up on my right, and when Ashton indicated for me to drive in, I did. What else was there to do? At least in a Little Chef, there would be people around even if it was just a couple of waitresses. I pulled up in front and got out. Ashton parked behind the Elf, presumably, so I couldn't get away. He got out and walked towards me.

"Where is Kristie?"

"She's a long way from here, and you've got no chance of getting to her, so don't waste your time."

He reached into his pocket, and I made a move to stop him. He stepped back and drew a packet of cigarettes from his jacket.

"I'm a Republican, but I'm not a killer." He offered me one. I shook my head, still trying to work out if I should hit him.

"She's taken you in the same as she took me in. I would have caught you sooner, but the bitch stole my car keys. I had to hot wire it to get the engine going. All I want to know is where she has gone that's all."

"Well, you've come to the wrong place, Ashton, or should I say, Harper. Not only did you use the girl's mother to make sex videos but then you try and sell her to a bunch of Arabs." As the words came out of my mouth, they didn't sound as convincing as when Kristie had said them a few hours ago, and Ashton's look of puzzlement was either great acting, or he didn't have a clue what I was talking about.

"I think we had better go inside and have a coffee, Shannon. It looks like you are a sucker for a pretty face and a sad story, just like me."

I followed him inside and ordered the full breakfast with extra toast and marmalade. It was that sort of a night

CHAPTER TWENTY-SIX

"Before you say anything or judge me, just listen, Mr Shannon. I only want a few minutes of your time."

I said nothing, but cut a piece of sausage and stuffed it into my mouth. I was so hungry that I found it difficult to concentrate. He had gone for the healthy option, of a pot of tea, a plain scone and yet another cigarette. I spread some thick Chivers Old-English Marmalade over my toast and listened. I still didn't trust the creep and was working out what to do with him when he eventually stopped bleating at me.

"Throughout the troubles in Northern Ireland, I have been a steadfast supporter of the fight for justice. I'm sick like a lot of Catholics of all the atrocities carried out by the British Army, especially the SAS and their undercover agents."

"OK Ashton, I get your political speech, just cut to the meat and veg please, before I start to cry and get out my violin."

"I have been a member of the movement all my life, my father was killed by the British and my mother committed suicide because of it. I have been a fundraiser for the last twenty years and have raised money all over the world for the cause. We get our money together, purchase diamonds and send them back to Ireland once a year from various disused airfields around Britain. Diamonds are easy to smuggle through customs, can be sold virtually anywhere in the world and rarely lose much of their value.

I met Kristie in New York. She was staying in the same hotel, and she introduced herself to me. She remembered me with her mother, though when I knew her, then she was just a child. Her mother was a patriot just like I am, and Kristie's real father had been killed by the UDA when Mary was carrying her. I never told her this, you understand, she already knew it. She said that she hated the English and wanted to do something to help the cause. She offered me £15000, and what could I do?"

"You took it?"

"Of course, I did, but then the inevitable happened, and we ended up in bed."

"Looking how old you are compared to her, I don't think it was that inevitable."

"She seduced me, Shannon. I swear it. She was a difficult girl to resist."

I couldn't argue with that. I poured out a cup of tea and blitzed it with sugar and milk. I needed the energy boost.

"I have a house here as you know, and when I came back, she practically moved in with me. She knew that I made videos and sometimes used her mother and wanted to know the truth about how she died. I handled the business end of the operation; I left the artistic side to Jenson."

"Jenson James?"

"He was another committed Republican; he was also into a lot of kinky stuff. In the end, he went too far."

"How do you mean?"

"They were supposed to be doing a video with him having sex with Kristie's mother, Mary while she was being strangled. It's supposed to be the ultimate orgasm. Anyway, it went horribly

wrong, and Mary died. Unfortunately, I let Jenson persuade me that

to sell the video would make a fortune for the cause. As it happened,

it did, but I guess Kristie didn't understand. Her mother would have

done for sure; she was a real professional. Jenson was wrong, but I

was stupid because I told Kristie what had happened, though she

seemed to understand. "

"She obviously didn't though," I said.

"No, she obviously didn't."

"So what's happened?"

"We went to the airfield with the diamonds. Kristie insisted on

coming. There were some associates flying in from Southern Ireland,

and my job was to hand over the goods. I had an estimated one-

hundred thousand pounds of gems on me when I arrived. We went

out to greet the plane, and I had what I thought were the diamonds

on me in a leather bag. When they were checked for authenticity, I

was told they were fakes. Kristie was nowhere to be seen, and we

had an argument by the side of the landing strip. Adam Sweet was shot and killed, and I was given 24 hours to get the stones back. I need to know where she is, Shannon. The men I am dealing with thought I was trying to rip them off, even if they wanted to, they couldn't let me get away with it."

"Isn't it your money anyway?"

"They fund my operation up front, and pay for the girls the camera crew......"

"Your jet-setting lifestyle?"

"That's right; my jet-setting lifestyle too."

I finished off my tea. "That's a good story, Ashton but I don't believe a word. If it is true, though, I think that the best thing for you to do is run."

"I'm dead if you don't tell me; you don't know what you are dealing with. There isn't anywhere to run. They will find me no matter where I go."

I got up from my seat. "I've heard enough. Even if I knew where she was heading, I wouldn't tell you. My advice is to disappear.

Now are you going to pull a gun and try to shoot me, or are you going to bugger off and leave me to get home? The tea and scone are on me." That was the least I could do.

Ashton left, a dejected man. Whether I believed him or not, I couldn't say, but I appreciated that I had been told two brilliant though contradictory stories during the course of the evening. I was still hungry, so I went over to the counter and looked at the menu.

"Can I order a cheese omelette?"

The girl looked up from her newspaper lazily, as if I was getting on her nerves just by being there. "Omelettes haven't arrived yet."

"Don't you just need a couple of eggs and some cheese?"

She looked at me as if I was mentally retarded, and carried on reading her paper.

I threw a note on the counter told her to forget it and headed out of the door. I suppose I was behind the times, or maybe the Little Chef was ahead of them, with their ready to microwave meals. If Shoddy was up when I got home, I would get him to crack a few eggs for me. I looked at my watch. It was coming up to seven

o'clock; home by half past eight and hopefully second breakfast by

nine.

CHAPTER TWENTY-SEVEN

It was Shoddy who threw light on the true story of what had been happening between Ashton and Kristie. After telling me how relieved he was that I wasn't one of the two bodies discovered in Anglesey by the police in the early hours of the morning, he sat me down in front of the TV pushed in the video and said, "Take a look at this."

"Isn't it a bit early for porn, Shod?"

"Just take a look."

He had fast-forwarded the video to the end, and as the credits rolled, I missed it the first time. He wound it back and told me to watch closely. I spotted it the second time around. The name of the man was something Polish and unpronounceable, but the name of the woman was one that I knew so well. Rose Black.

"That girl, what was she called?"

"Alisha Lee."

"Right. That girl, Alisha Lee, didn't get it wrong; she was trying to tell you the name of the actress. It's my guess that Kristie's mum had a false stage name. What was her real maiden name?"

"I don't know her surname, but her first name was Mary."

"So that was more than likely Rosemary. It can be shortened either way to Mary or Rose.

As Shoddy cooked my second breakfast, I told him about the events of the night before. I still couldn't believe that Kristie was the black rose killer, but everything pointed that way, and I felt like an idiot for believing the tale that she had spun me. Shoddy was more philosophical, saying that it could have happened to anyone.

Where Kristie was and where she was going to I had no idea, but the thought that this innocent girl could be a cold blooded murderer was hard to believe. The facts spoke for themselves, though. She had killed Jenson out of revenge and Charlie for self-preservation. She had even left the letter for me to follow her to the airfield, and for all I know was holding a gun to his head when he left the message on my answer phone.

Life wasn't as cut and dried as fiction, but there were too many loose ends in this case for my liking, and I didn't know what I was going to tell Henry Green. For Nina Page also, the road ended here, and possibly she would now never find out who Harper was and why he had killed her husband, Rudi.

A couple of days later, one part of the case was well and truly cleared up by Shoddy. He asked one of his police colleagues to give him some information about the shootings on the island of Anglesey. The two men had been identified as Charlie Steel, a private detective from London, and Adam Sweet a Merseyside Nightclub owner. Sweet had been shot through the kneecaps and the head.

The body of a man later identified by police as Ashton Baxter had been found in a black Cosworth in the long-term car park at Liverpool airport. He also had been kneecapped and shot through the head, which led the police to believe that it was an IRA killing. Neither Sweet nor Baxter had any roses, black or otherwise stuck in their mouths.

One of the problems that I had about Kristie was the note left in the cottage in Anglesey for me to follow. Why did she leave that? Shoddy reasoned that she didn't know if I would come, but by leaving the note, at least if I did she would know where to find me. As a concept, it was brilliant, but was she really that smart? Shoddy said that in his opinion she was. If I came, then she could use me, if I didn't, then she would have stolen the Cosworth. Part of being a professional and staying alive was the attention to detail, and Kristie seemed to have mastered this brilliantly. However, her callousness was depressing.

EPILOGUE

The facts of the case kept drifting in during the weeks that followed. A lot of these facts were due to Shoddy's determination and sheer grit to get to the truth. Kristie had killed Jenson James for performing and then selling the video of the fatal sex act with her mother. However, there was another motive. Apparently, he had discovered that the money in the trust fund set up by Kristie's mother was not enough to fund Henry Green's first-class lifestyle. The rest of the money was coming from somewhere else. That somewhere and the final piece in the jigsaw was revealed in a letter sent to me by Nina Page, who had now gone back home.

Dear Mr Shannon,

I have been meaning to write to you and offer my gratitude for your help in tracking down my husband's killer. The man called Harper. I enclose a copy of the last report sent to me by Charlie Steel. He sent me this from Paris, a day before he was so brutally murdered. I hope this will help clear up the mystery for you as it has done for me.

Best wishes

Nina Page

Report: From Charlie Steel to Nina Page 23rd August 1986
Paris

*As per my message last night, I took the flight to Paris and went
to see three of the staff of the Excelsior hotel in the Puteaux district
of the city.*

*I brought with me several pictures taken of Ashton Baxter in the
hope of a formal identification of who Harper is. Two of the staff
said that they didn't recognise Ashton, but a receptionist clearly
identified Kristie Green.*

*This leads me to conclude that we have been looking at the wrong
person and that in fact, Kristie Green is or rather was Harper, the
person who killed your husband. At this moment in time, I cannot say
why black roses were placed in the mouths of the victims. However, I
am 100 percent certain that what seemingly is an innocent looking
girl is in fact, an international killer and fraudster of the highest*

level, and as such should be treated with caution. I strongly advise

you to stay in the house with the doors locked until I return.

I will investigate further and report back after my trip to

Anglesey.

Keep safe,

Charlie

THE END

Thank you for reading the Penny Detective. If you enjoyed it, pass it on and tell some of your friends. If you want to contact me with any comments, ideas or thoughts about the book, or just for a chat, look me up on:

Facebook: https://www.facebook.com/john.t.jones.52

Twitter: https://twitter.com/john151253.

Email me at john151253@gmail.com to go on my mailing list for information about new books coming out. I never divulge any information to a third party.

I always reply and am always very happy to hear from you.

Other books in the Penny Detective series are:

1. The Penny Detective

2. The Italian Affair

3. An Evening with Max Climax

4. The Shoestring Effect

5. Chinese Whispers

6. Murder at Bewley Manor

7. Dead Man Walking

8. The Hangman Mystery

9. Flawed

Before you go, here are a couple of chapters from book 9 in the Penny Detective series; Flawed.

SPRING 1987

CHAPTER ONE

I'd been working on an insurance fraud case for a couple of weeks that had taken me to London and then on to Hastings and Brighton. The work was straightforward enough, and I now had a cheque in my pocket that would pay the rent for a while and keep me in beer and chips. I finished the contract on the Friday afternoon, and in gratitude for a job well done, was given the option of spending the rest of the weekend at the hotel I'd been working from, at the insurance company's expense. I was eating a medium-rare fillet steak that evening when on an impulse I decided to head for home. After three weeks of two-star hotel bedrooms and dining in Wimpy Bars, I was tired. I was tired of greasy crap food and having to talk to shady insurance fraudsters and pretend I was part of the scam.

I got up from the table, went to my room and packed my stuff into my kit bag. I checked out, and twenty minutes later was on the A23 heading north and home. At that time of night, traffic was light, and I didn't expect there to be any delays on the M1 as I pointed the nose of my Riley Elf towards Merseyside and Croxley. The drive would have normally taken around five hours, but in the end took me nine as I fell asleep in the Hilton Park Services near Wolverhampton.

By the time I eventually arrived in Croxley it was a little after six, and I was wide awake after eating a huge breakfast and washing it down with two mugs of strong, but pretty bad tasting, motorway coffee. I decided to go into the office before going home and then retire for the rest of the day for a well-earned rest in bed.

I stayed longer in the office than I had expected, opening bills and listening to three weeks of answer phone messages before the machine ran out of tape. By the time I pulled into the car park in front of my flat, I was depressed. The news from the office wasn't very uplifting, just bills, complaints, and no offers of work. Already I had changed plans and decided to hit the pub for the rest of the day instead of the sack. On days like these, the only alternative was to get blind stinking drunk and then dull the brain with some serious afternoon TV and a mega pack of cheese and onion crisps.

It was a bright and clear February morning, though the clouds moving in from behind the gasworks were tinged black and looked ominous. It was good to be back in Croxley, even though it had only been three weeks, and I drank in the smell of rotting Chinese takeaways in the huge grey bins that were littered around the car park, mingled with the aroma of petrol, vomit, and dog shit. The fragrance I was used to; the sweet smell of home.

A stunning young girl wearing black hot pants and a skin tight beige blouse opened the door of number six, which had been empty for a couple of months. She looked about 20 and had dyed white hair that was cut into a pageboy style and huge cat-green eyes. She had an unlit cigarette in one hand and an overnight bag in the other.

"Have you got a light for this?" She said.

I shook my head and then remembered the car cigarette lighter. "Hang on a minute, Luv; you can use the one in the car."

She left the flat door open, put the bag down, and came towards me with exaggerated hip movements as if she enjoyed the fact that my eyes were popping out of my head. She passed me the cigarette, and I lit and gave it to her back.

She didn't seem to be in a hurry to go anywhere.

"You're that detective bloke aren't you?" She had a slight Welsh accent.

I nodded and wondered how she knew. "And you're that Welsh girl aren't you?" I was trying to be funny, but it fell flat, and she didn't pick up on my lame attempt at humour. That probably was because it wasn't very witty. I tried a more direct approach.

"So what's your name?"

"Nancy; that's Nancy Hendrix and no, I'm not related."

She'd lost me and must have seen the confusion on my face because she added. "Jimi Hendrix? People always ask me when I first meet them, if I am his sister."

"And are you?"

"No, you daft bugger; but I've got a couple of his records."

A man got out of a car across the street and headed into the car park. He was wearing a light blue lounge suit, with a sleeveless anorak. He was going bald, had a pencil moustache, and looked like a spiv. As he approached, he shouted, "Get your skates on, Nancy, I want an early start." The car park was getting kind of busy now, even though it was still early. Another woman stepped through the door of number six and made her way over. This one had dark hair done up in a ponytail and looked like an older version of the girl I'd been talking to.

As the man approached, Nancy dropped the half-smoked cigarette onto the floor and hastily stamped it out with her foot. For no apparent reason, she looked worried. If she was pleased with the arrival of either the man or the woman, it didn't show on her face. The man walked up and gave her a kiss, then pointed his head in my direction. "Who's your big friend, doll?"

"That's some man from one of the upstairs flats, Shane."

The man pushed his head forward into her face in an aggressive manner. "What have I told you about smoking?"

"I ain't been smoking."

"I can smell it on your breath and all over your clothes."

"What's wrong with a smoke now and again, Shane? You're a fucking control freak. You'd better try treating her with a bit more respect or she's gonna start rebelling."

Shane, who looked like a right pain in the arse, turned his attention away from Nancy and laid into the woman who had just made the comment. She was standing with her hands on her hips staring at him.

"So what do you mean by that? ' Start rebelling?' Are you trying to put thoughts into her head out of spite?"

"No; but Nancy has got a brain of her own, and she doesn't need a wanker like you telling her what she can or can't do."

His glance moved lazily in my direction. "So who do you say Nancy's friend is, again?"

"How the hell do I know, I've never set eyes on him before, but looking at the way he's dressed he could be plain clothes police, so you'd better watch your mouth."

That stopped Shane for a couple of seconds, and he looked me up and down, taking in my crumpled suit and threadbare trilby. "You look more like an insurance salesman, mate. Are we holding you up?

Or is there something here that has taken your fancy." He looked at Nancy then back at me.

Shane was beginning to get up my nose, and I felt like punching him but didn't have the energy. Thankfully, he ignored me and spoke to Nancy. "Let's get out of here, doll, it's a long drive, and I want to miss the rush hour traffic."

"Doll?" He couldn't be serious.

Nancy looked at the older woman, mouthed, "See ya," then picked up her overnight bag and walked off with Shane. We both watched as they headed for the street. There was a Silver Mercedes parked in front of a boarded up newsagents. They got in, and seconds later, it pulled away with an exaggerated squeal of rubber.

"Tosser," I said under my breath

The woman came over. "Sorry about that, he's an idiot."

I shrugged, "Unfortunately, there's a lot of them about in Croxley, but don't apologise, it's not your fault."

She seemed to think that I needed an explanation for his behaviour, but the truth was that I didn't give a damn and just wanted to get back to my place and close the door.

"He's always been aggressive ever since we met him, but he's a flash bugger, and unfortunately, Nancy has fallen for all of the shit that he's been feeding her."

"I take it you don't like him."

"Can't stand the man, but he seems to have some power over her, and that's that. There is nothing I can do about it. I'm Stella by the way, Nancy's sister." She added with a half smile." That's older sister."

"Older but wiser?" I quipped

She gave me a dazzling smile. "I've made my fair share of mistakes, I'm afraid. That's why I can spot a loser like Nancy's fella, a mile off.

I held out my hand, and she took it. "I'm Morris, but my friends call me Moggsy. I live upstairs."

"Yeah, I know all about you, Morris, I was talking to your partner. He said you were away on a case down in London. It sounded all very James Bond and exciting. Like something out of a movie. I've just made some tea; do you want to come in?"

The offer was tempting, but at that moment, all I needed was sleep as my recent burst of energy seemed to have deserted me. "Do you mind if I pass on that, Stella. I've just driven from the south coast, and I need to get some rest."

She looked genuinely disappointed, and I instantly wished that I had accepted. I could see that not only was she an older version of her sister, but she was a much classier model. She didn't have the dyed hair or the sexy clothes, but she was pretty enough to make me wish I had cleaned my teeth and had a wash before getting so close.

If she was genuinely sad that I didn't take her up on the offer, she recovered quickly and gave me a half-hearted resigned smile. She said, "Some other time then," Winked sexily at me, went back into her flat and closed the door.

I made my way up the stairs to my flat, not wanting to risk the temperamental lift. I let myself in and collapsed fully clothed on the bed.

CHAPTER TWO

"I tell you Moggsy; I'm definitely on with that tart in number six. She was all over me the other day; I couldn't get rid of her."

"Are you sure she doesn't think you've got money?" I was sitting in my partner Shoddy's flat, which just happened to be next door to mine. It was a couple of days after my spur of the moment return to Croxley, and I was watching him cook bacon and eggs for our breakfast. The fact that he thought Stella Hendrix had the hots for him was highly amusing, and I didn't have the heart to burst his dreams. He was a terrific bloke with a razor sharp mind for solving problems, but he did have some seriously severe flaws in his personality and appearance.

Shoddy was a raging alcoholic and had the sort of derelict bodily appearance that started at the top with his grey receding hairline and got worse as your eyes worked their way down. A bulbous red boozer's nose, missing front teeth, nicotine stained fingers and a permanent odour of ready rubbed tobacco, and cheap cider gave him a certain exclusivity that I doubted would attract a woman like

Stella. He was dressed in an old brown cardigan, with buttons missing, a blue and white striped polyester pyjama top and urine stained shabby grey trousers. His appearance usually had the effect of driving people away, and I hoped that he wasn't going to embarrass himself with our new neighbours.

"I'd stay well clear of that one if I were you, Shod."

"Oh yeah, why is that?"

"I don't think she's your type."

He dished out the bacon and eggs onto the plates, buttered toast and brought over a couple of mugs of tea. He sat down at the table and mulled over what I had just said. "I was going to ask her to come up and have a drink this Saturday."

"Bad move, Shoddy. We don't know anything about her or her sister. I reckon that she's got the whiff of somebody who has got a husband tucked away somewhere. You don't want that sort of aggro."

"Are you sure that you're not sniffing around her yourself?"

"Course not. You know me, Shod; I'd never try to move in on a mate's woman. No, it's just that I don't think that she's right for you. You need somebody a bit more intelligent."

"So, are you saying she's not very clever?"

"No, I'm not saying that. What I'm saying is that maybe you don't have anything in common."

He shovelled some eggs and bacon into his mouth, took a swig of tea and burped. "I haven't had a woman up here...........Well, never really. Did you know that, Moggsy? The only person that has ever been in that bedroom is me. I just get a bit lonely sometimes."

I was just about to answer him when there was a knock on the door. It made us both jump as Shoddy very rarely had any visitors. We both sat there staring in the general direction of where the noise had come from, and whoever it was knocked again.

Shoddy took another swig of tea, got up and walked over to the door. Rather than open it, he shouted, "Hello, who is it?"

"It's Stella from number six."

He turned around to me with a huge toothless grin on his face and gave me the thumbs up sign. He reached into his pocket, slipped his dentures into his mouth, and put his thumbs up again.

She then added, "I'm looking for Morris. I've just knocked his door, but he's not in. I was wondering if he was with you."

That wiped the smile off his face, and he seemed to deflate in front of me as he opened the door. When she saw me, she totally ignored Shoddy and talked over his shoulder. "I'm glad I found you, Morris. I need to have a word if that's possible."

You'd better come in," said Shoddy.

She looked at him for the first time. "In private," she said sternly.

"Can you give me a couple of minutes to finish breakfast, and I will come down."

She gave a wave in my general direction and disappeared down the corridor. Shoddy slammed the door, sat down again and continued eating in silence.

It looked as if I had been right about Stella Hendrix being trouble; nothing like a beautiful woman to come between a detective and his partner. And talking about beautiful girlfriends. My very fit and posh companion, Lady Cynthia Laval, was still on holiday in the Caribbean with her rich 'Cheshire Set' friends. I could have been sitting on some white beach now and staying with her and her cousin the Third Duke of Ipswich. That fact that he thought that the definition of working class was anyone that had a house with less than twenty bedrooms was one of the reasons I didn't go with her. To be honest, I prefer the freezing cold and damp conditions in Croxley to sitting in a beach bar in Antigua with Lady C and her friends, poking fun at the natives. The fact that I had a girlfriend, and he didn't was always an issue that Shoddy liked to push in my face from time to time. Maybe a girlfriend would be a good thing for him, but I hardly thought that a girl like Stella was going to give him a second look. In my experience, beautiful women like her were more trouble than they were worth, and I wondered what particular kind of trouble she was going to lay at my door. Whatever it was, I hoped that she intended to pay for my help.

Made in the USA
Lexington, KY
19 April 2017